ABSENCE

Sarah Paton Wiseman

HOPCYN PRESS

Published by Hopcyn Press Limited

Hopcyn Press
42 Russell Rd
London W14 8HT
Tel: +44 (0) 20 7371 6488
Email: info@hopcynpress.com
www.hopcynpress.com

ISBN: 978-0-9928933-7-8

For Brigid Keenan
whose enthusiasm, advice and support are ever-present in ABSENCE

ACKNOWLEDGEMENTS

I would like to thank my publisher and editor Marguerite Evers for her encouragement and help, practical and creative. I am grateful to my Irish friends: Sally Keane, Bill and Daphne Montgomery and the late Robin Chichester-Clark for their houses, humour, hills, kitchens and knowledge of their country which is an inspiration to me. I am grateful to my daughter Alix and to Harriet Bridgeman for tirelessly reading everything I write. Adrian Dawney has been especially helpful with literature pertaining to cults. I thank Sheona Stewart for her invaluable, professional advice regarding elective and selective mutes. Special thanks, too, to Nigel Smith who faithfully untangles every computer crisis. I appreciate the wonderful encouragement of friends and family and also remember absent friends, whose presence in my life inspired me to write this book.

CHAPTER
1

MISS BLANE

The precise span between the wheels of Mother's chair was twenty inches and the width of the cliff path that leads steeply up the hill above Ballygore Bay is uneven, somewhere between sixteen and thirty inches. I was having a time of it, pushing the wheelchair up the dusky path. Halfway to the top I looked down and saw the sea below, spluttering like a pot on the boil. Good enough, but I kept going. It would give more satisfaction from the top.

I pushed on, heaving it over stones, cramming it through the narrow bits. I'd strapped her intimate apparel onto the seat, the things that still had her powdery smell about them. From time to time I'd get a whiff of her, stronger than the stinging sea air. I reached the top, panting to be sure, but filled with elation. Then I pushed . . .

Ah, but you should have seen it go, somersaulting through the air like a live thing. It smashed against the rocks, once, twice, before the sea reached up and sucked it down into the water. Only her dressing gown, the silk one trimmed with crêpe de chine, loosened itself from the chair and clung to a rock, shivering and sodden, before the next wave tore it down.

It was a job well done, although I have to admit, she beat me to the post. It could have been *her*, her inside the dressing gown, hurtling down the cliff with all her powders and paints and knickers and nighties. She was light enough to hurtle. The same smash, the same waves, one little grey foot sailing off by itself into the sea she so despised. Ah, that would have been perfection!

"An accident," they would have said. "The dressmaker's faithful daughter taking her mother for a breath of sea air.' 'What with the state of the path . . ."

No, she won the day, dying in her own bed that very afternoon, still nothing could hold me back now. After twenty years of slavery I was for college and a new life!

★   ★   ★

It came at last, feebleness and fear. The doctor's search for a vein in her spider limbs. But even in those last hours she had me by her side taking down instructions. She was to be laid out on cream – coloured satin, no matter the price. I was to see she had her best knickers on and the slip from Lyon. She wanted to be dressed in her linen suit with my grandmother's ruby brooch at her throat.

"Who was my father?" I asked, "Tell me now!"

She didn't answer. I was to see the skirt wasn't crumpled It was the one chance a lady got to wear linen without it crumpling.

"Who was my father?" I raised my voice. "I'll crumple the linen I'll sell the brooch."

She stared up at me with hate in her eyes.

"Respectable; a respectable gentleman, business to attend to . . ."

"What business? Where?"

"Toady!" her name for me came out in a diminished whine, "Show me again my pretty, pretty things."

"My father?" I cried.

A drowning gurgle came from her throat.

★   ★   ★

She died at four p.m., missing her tea in the Spode cup she'd bought off one of her ladies at a charity sale. By six-thirty she was in the morgue without her brooch, laid out on a good plain sheet. By five after nine in the evening her chair was somersaulting through the air into with her beloved *pretty* things into the broiling sea.

Life moves on. I've myself to think of now that I'm on my own, set for a fresh start, on my way to becoming a professional.

★   ★   ★

Two years later I had completed my training. I was registered with a proper agency as an Assistant Social Worker. A framed diploma in Child Development hung over my bed. The letters ASW have a fine ring to them, not to be sneezed at, not at all

I won't say the training wasn't onerous, what with learning to work the computer and the speed the younger ones work at. I'd a few of the exams to take over, but I didn't lose heart. Then, only three weeks later, I was offered my first job – the school, right here in Ballyloe, County Cork, was after an ASW to provide additional support to a family with an eight year old girl, diagnosed as an elective mute. An Elective Mute! Make no mistake; mutism is a speciality, not a common learning disorder like dyslexia. My agency was recommended and it was *me* they chose. It would have been me they had their eye on from the start, what with my maturity and sensible approach. I have to smile when I think of those floozies who were with me at college with A levels coming out of their . . . well, I'm not one to look down on anyone, but aren't they the ones still scurrying around looking for work in institutions? While I was the one landed a job?

And you'd never guess which family it was – the Gowries up at Cleary Court, no less. It's a grand house outside the town, one of the grandest around these parts. I'm over the moon!

When Maisie's case history arrived there was a curious warning at the end:

Do not underestimate the fact that the Gowrie family is suffering the loss of their only son, Maisie's brother, Owen. He has been classified as a missing person since he disappeared in the summer of 2010.

It's a strange enough story. Haven't we all read about it in the newspapers and heard it talked about at Tilly's shop? It seems that the boy was studying up at the university in Dublin, and then from one day to the next he was gone. Not dead; not found again; just GONE.

But what did he have to do with me? Nothing! It's the little girl I've been called upon to help. I was back at my books right away, revising the right approach. Sure and I'll have her talking in no time.

I was to meet Mrs Gowrie and the child the following Tuesday. I considered wearing my pale blue suit, the one I wore at my graduation ceremony. But in the end I favoured a county look. I went to Mother's cupboard and took out her best tweed jacket; it's Donegal tweed, lined in fine silk cut on the bias with a velvet cord collar. I keep her fine things, you see. I keep them brushed and steamed. She had her turn, flaunting about in them before the accident. She had a youth: scent and silk stockings and men calling. Some people are allowed a youth, others aren't. From the age of fourteen Mother had me tethered like a goat on a short rope.

I tried on the jacket with my black slacks. "Too tight, Toad," I could hear Mother say. "Out! Let it out . . . you're a sight for sore eyes." Ha! Let her complain all she likes under the sod, I thought. "She can't get at me now." I smiled at myself in the mirror. I adjusted my smile and fluffed up my hair. I wound a scarf round my neck for flare. I was ready for a bit of flare. I thought I looked fine; not fancy mind, but quite the part.

I had another glance at the warning. It would be well over a year ago since the lad went missing. Why should I care?

★   ★   ★

The house – what a shock! I'd expected a handsome gate and a long drive like the ones in the Merchant-Ivory films, but I could hardly get up the path. It was choking with wild fuchsia, nettles and gone-to-seed vegetables. There were broken slates, fallen from the roof, no doubt, and a donkey was wandering free.

There wasn't a soul about so I walked through the open door and stood in the hall. An enormous painting was hanging there – a foreign town with canals running through it. It might have been Spain . . . or Italy, perhaps? Worth a packet once, I'd say, but nobody had paid the least mind to it. The canvas flapped free at the bottom and there was the remains of a bird's nest settled in the bottom corner of the frame.

Then, all of a sudden, *she* came down the stairs – Lila Gowrie! I know her well enough now alright. I'll admit I couldn't take my eyes off her. She was lovely to look at, wearing low-cut jeans, an oiled belt with a silver buckle and a T-shirt – too tight you'd think for a mother. But it was her eyes that held me, not Irish eyes, not the pure blue eyes we are blessed with around here, they were dark and foreign looking, beautiful in their way, but with something metallic in them, like the slice of a knife in butter.

When she spoke it was the same thing, a low voice, seductive you might say, but with a blade in there that could cut you down like a reaper.

"I'm the social worker, Mrs Gowrie," I said. "I'm here to meet Maisie."

"Ah yes," she said vaguely, as though she'd happened on me by chance. "Well, come along then."

I followed her into the drawing room. There was something strange about her walk. It was graceful, yet unsteady. She sat down on a sofa I can only describe as wasted. It would have been damask once, but the vermilion threads that showed were covered with animal hairs. They taught us the importance of a bright, clean environment at the college. It wasn't right at all. I took note of it and perched uncomfortably on the nearest chair, with a tabby cat taking up the greater part. Then, without so much as the offer of a cup of tea, she started in:

"You'll have heard, no doubt, that Maisie's not a great one for conversation? Choosy about whom she talks to, you might say."

There was a glitter of a smile. Her tone was amused, as though the subject were amusing.

"I'm aware of her condition . . ." I began. But she sailed on as though I didn't exist.

"There's only three of us she talks to, Miss . . . ?

"Blane."

"Blane, if you will." She said dismissively.

"Who is it she talks to then?" I asked politely.

"There's my elder daughter, Flora, who, it has to be said, is not a good influence."

She paused, drumming her fingers against the arm of the sofa. Her rings slid up and down her third finger. What gave her the right to be so stuck up, I wondered. I was feeling the heat. I loosened my silk scarf and gathered myself. She was only the mother after all. I was the professional.

"And the others?" I asked.

"Me, of course."

"Of course."

Up until then she hadn't looked at me directly. Now, suddenly, her eyes were on me, stripping me down.

"The third person my daughter talks to is not, not to all intents and purposes that is, actually present. Do you have experience with people that aren't present, Miss Blane? Do you?"

"Well, I've been advised . . ."

"No! I thought not," she interrupted. "Well, it's a relevant detail, a detail you might like to take into consideration before you meet my daughter."

There was an awkward silence.

"*Ella es la bendita de Dios!*" She suddenly burst out, raising her eyes to heaven. Then, seeing my bewildered expression, she explained in a patronizing voice, "What I mean is she's more fortunate than the rest of us. She converses with her brother."

Mother of God, what could a person say to that? Her eyes were black, with the hard shine of taffeta. I found I could hardly breathe under Mother's jacket. It was too tight after all.

"Now I don't want you to take that away from her. Do you understand? Whatever they say at her school . . ."

At that very moment the child Maisie appeared in the doorway. She was smaller than I'd expected, pale as a pear, with tousled hair the colour of barley. Her eyes were light, a clear bluish-green, proper Irish eyes. I smiled and held out my hand. She remained where she was, looking at us with a solemn expression. Lila Gowrie got up and turned on her heel with a flash of diamanté-studded sandal strap.

"Don't forget what I've told you!" she said to me over her

shoulder as she went out, leaving me alone with the little girl, discomfited.

I'd heard that warning before. It was to do with the boy again. I will say, I confess to it now, I paid it no mind at the time.

FLORA

Get this! She's into concussion this month. Suddenly it's obvious; we're all about to find him in a dear little nursing home with freshly washed sheets and a white floor. There'll be one faithful nurse who's been tending him all this time without wages for love of his long, slim body and his fair Irish hair. Owen always got things done for love. Anyway, our mother will sit by his bed and stroke his arm and say his name in that gorgeous voice she used to have before she went hysterical and, guess what? His eyelashes will flutter once, twice, and he'll open his blue, blue eyes and smile and say, "What's for dinner, Ma?" just like they do in the movies.

As if! Yeah, right, like angels exist and babies come from God on High instead of a randy lad and a girl who's forgotten to take the pill. Have they ever got things wrong at St Ursula's!

And now, on top of a disappeared brother and a totally mad mother, I've got a detention, just for asking Miss Brenda a few questions in Scripture.

If a man have an hundred sheep, and one of them be gone astray, doth he not leave the ninety and nine, and goeth into the mountains, and seeketh that which is gone astray.

I put up my hand. "S'pose that lamb took off just for the hell of it?"

"Flora!" she warned, her lips stitched together in disapproval. But it's a subject I'm into – so I spelled it out for her.

"Suppose it's just making trouble for the rest of the flock?" I explained. "I mean the ninety and nine? When they could be getting on with playing or growing up or moving to a better pasture? Like the shepherd's on that one lamb's case and he's probably left the rest of them with some useless collie and the mother sheep are . . ."

"Flora Gowrie," she interrupted, pink with anger. "Stop this blasphemy immediately. You know the symbolism well enough. It means our Lord takes care of each one of us, however frail, however pitiful."

Another detention! Not that I care . . . not that they do either. The parents don't check anymore. Of course I know the symbolism, but there's been too much seeking in our family. My father, Dad, well he has *sought* and *sought* for our lost lamb.

★ ★ ★

Mr Breen LLD is the lawyer my parents are crazy enough to trust. Actually, I'm not sure Dad trusts him as much as he did, but he's loyal. He *thinks* he's doing his best. As for Ma she'll cling to any old string and she's not great at judging strings; a blurred photograph of the back of a blond head that looks faintly familiar and she's on the telephone to Breen. He pretends to follow up on every back of every blond head to keep her happy. It does not keep her happy. Soon she's off on some new trail and on at him again.

This guy's been employed to find my brother ever since he cleared out over a year and a half ago. But bigoted old Breen hasn't a clue; for one thing he has a bee in his bonnet about politics. It buzzes endlessly round his right-wing, retarded brain making sums that go like this: Owen was at university. University students are all lefties. Lefties take off and cause trouble. Any trouble spot that has Irish students in it must have Owen Gowrie in it too: 0 plus 0 = 0.

It would help if he had any idea what my brother was like. Well, it might not help. If we can't work it out he certainly can't, but he thinks he's the new James Bond and stumbles around finding the wrong blood-stained handkerchief in the wrong sand.

In fact something massive did happen to Owen when he was thirteen. His best friend Billy Doherty was a tough little boy with red curly hair, brilliant at football and running, the opposite of my brother. Owen was a Peter Pan sort of child, fair and thin and useless at games, except for make-believe ones. He didn't get into fights if he could help it and he wasn't into shooting. He refused point blank to put a ferret down after a rabbit – quite rare with Irish boys who often have a ferret on them.

I was only little then, but I remember Owen and Billy together fooling around doing normal things like fishing and making fires with Dad's magnifying glass. They used to fun-wrestle. I remember that especially, because Owen wasn't strong and Billy was. They'd tackle each other and roll over and over laughing. I was impressed because Owen often won. Now I realize Billy probably let him.

I was dead envious when Owen was invited to go to Donegal with the Dohertys the year he was twelve. Billy's father was a well-off farmer with four sons, all mad about fly-fishing. Our parents hardly knew them and they certainly didn't have the faintest idea about Mick, an older brother who was in trouble. Donegal is where our parents met. They are soppy about things like that and, to Dad, anyone who loves fishing is perfect, so they said yes.

Owen came back that first time ecstatic. He described climbing up to a place called the Lough of the Fat Trout and walking through a mysterious Poisoned Glen. He'd been to a mountain called Errigal which was ex-volcanic: 'If it had erupted mega huge flames and molten lava would have shot out and we'd have been preserved like mummies', he said. 'What are mummies?' I asked. 'It means we'd have lasted forever,' he explained with a touch of superiority. It sounded wonderful. I was six at the time and didn't know what molten lava was.

Owen's stories grew and altered and took flight like starlings. Maisie and I thought they were better than books.

The next year he was invited again. By that time he was good acasting and Dad had taught him how to tie a Teal and Blue and a Hare's Ear. I remember him leaving, crushed into the back of a green Land Rover with the Doherty boys. A dinghy was strapped to the roof and fishing rods stuck out of the windows. Owen was white with excitement, too excited to wave.

But five days later he was back. I was told there had been a terrible accident. Nobody would say what the terrible accident was, but I could tell something strange and awful had happened to my brother. He locked the door of his room and wouldn't let anyone in. We could hear him banging his head against the wall. Dad and Ma pleaded with him to let them in. He wouldn't. The head-thudding went on and on . . . finally they must have broken the lock. Ma spent all night in his room.

Billy Doherty was dead.

Dad told me later that a man had burst into Billy's uncle's farmhouse. Mick Doherty, the one they were after, was shot in the chest, but survived. We still don't know what he'd done – I mean whether he'd been in the IRA or was an informer against it or who exactly was after him. But Billy died, caught in the line of fire trying to protect his brother. And Owen was *there* . . . he was under the kitchen table in his pyjamas too scared to move. He must have seen everything, blood everywhere and Mick being carried out to an ambulance. He must've heard the keening and seen sheets, a sheet put over dear Billy's face. That would have been the worst bit.

The next day Owen came out of his room pale and clinging to Dad. I followed them downstairs. Two policemen were sitting at our kitchen table.

"How is it you didn't know about Mick Doherty, Mr Gowrie?"

"How is it you let your lad go to Donegal with that family, sir?"

"Is the name McGinley familiar to you."

"Would the names Donal and Callum Glyn mean anything to you?"

Dad didn't know a thing, of course, but he was flustered all the same.

"We only knew the child," he kept repeating. "It was the fishing, you see. They invited my son for the fishing . . ."

"Sure and you'll have heard about the Doherty family's involvement in the kidnapping up at Belton Tower, sir?"

"No! I mean, yes! I mean, I read about the kidnapping – but I'd no idea it was them. We didn't know them then, you see. And how can you tell? How can anyone tell who is with them and who isn't?"

"By the singing, sir. 'Tis the pubs they sing in and t'nature of the songs tells you which of the lads are in with the IRA."

When they started firing questions at Owen Dad held him tightly, shielding his face with his hand, as if the shooting was still going on.

Nothing terrible had happened to us before so we didn't know what to do. I cried when Ma cried, but it wasn't real crying. When I think about Billy now it's a blur. I just remember he often had warm sweets in his pockets for me and Maisie.

Of course it changed Owen, but it's hard to say how. He *seemed* alright – after a bit. He adored Maisie and I think he loved me, we were normal together. Well, Owen was more or less normal . . .

To get back to Breen, the day he found out about Billy was a field day for him, just the sort of thing that turns him on. The way he saw it Owen had to be after vengeance. If there's a hint of trouble anywhere: Latin America, the Middle East, any old country in Africa, he sniffs around till he finds out if European kids have been there, not peace-keeping ones, forget it! Our lawyer's fixated on the idea of junior mercenaries, baby bomb makers, the sort who like the feel a Kalashnikov slung over their shoulder, boys that are longing to crawl through jungles on their stomachs, setting people free from oppressive governments.

Right! Forgive me for laughing at your sleuthing skills Mr B but Owen hasn't got a drop of vengeance in his veins. He wouldn't even shoot clay pigeons after Billy's death. He doesn't like bangs. He's a pacifist and he never eats meat, not even Ma's bacon. She used to cook it glistening with butter and honey and sprinkled with cinnamon crumbs smelling of . . . God! But the smell of it would drive you wild, but my brother is a vegetarian.

★   ★   ★

The first thing our lawyer organized for Dad, only two months after he was hired, was a trip to Gaza. His reasoning was that the situation out there had attracted subversive kids from other countries who thought they were helping the Arab cause. And, since he considered our brother was obviously subversive, he thought he might be there. That spring, Mairead Corrigan-Maguire, one of the human rights activists fighting against the Israeli blockade, was put into prison in Ramallah and when she reported that other Irish nationals were there too, that did it for him. He was on at Dad to leave with him as soon as possible.

I wouldn't put Breen down as pro-Jewish, no way! But he certainly isn't into the Islamic thing. He's the sort who thinks the

Israelis must be right because the USA supports them and the Arabs must be wrong because they look weird. I absolutely can't see him in the desert. I bet he hates skin that isn't pink and Irish like his.

Our father's view wasn't the same as Breen's, but he couldn't ignore the possibility that Owen *might* have got involved because of Mairead. It's true he might. He'd met her after a lecture at university. She's the best protester we've got, massively brave and peace-loving. She won the Nobel Peace Prize during the Troubles. She's been aboard ships with pro-Palestinians trying to get into Gaza harbour with medicine and drinking water – stuff the people desperately need. My parents knew how passionate Owen was about injustice – they knew he admired Mairead . . .

That was enough for them – that's the mad part! People who live on hope weave shapes out of thin air, then they breathe life into the shapes. I was doing it too then, hoping with them, believing with them – putting my trust in woven air.

Three people travelled to Gaza: the lawyer, my father and a single parent mother from Cork called Maureen O'Neill whose only child Rory had been missing for longer than Owen. The plan was they'd stay in a hotel and search for their missing people from there. Breen was to set up interviews with helpful people. It was a dangerous time. They were warned to stay in the hotel.

But my father didn't stay in the hotel. He wouldn't have been on for an internet search – he's never Googled in his life. He would have wanted to look for his son himself, with his own two loving Irish eyes. He likes walking and looking; that's what he's used to.

He could have been killed. It would have been Owen's fault if he had been.

Look, none of us know what happened. Dad was there for over two weeks and when he came back he looked as if he'd been in the war himself. He hardly mentions Gaza now . . . only once, on a walk, he told me a muddled story about a man called Jamil who offered to help him to find Owen. He told me Jamil's family were living in half a shop . . . a bomb had fallen on the other half, killing his wife and one child. There were other kids in the house – a little girl with splinters of glass in her stomach.

How our father got caught up in all this I've no idea, but somehow he ended up helping the man who was supposed to be helping him. When I asked questions he shut up. He does this, starts something, then cuts off and lapses into silence.

Breen's journey was not a success. He failed to find any trace of either boy. All he'd managed to prove was that they weren't dead, not dead in Gaza, anyway.

★   ★   ★

Our lost lamb took off ages ago – and look at us now! Dad's skipped years, he shuffles and keeps his head down. And Ma, our beautiful mother, drinks. It's not her fault. I've read about it – stress leads unwittingly to alcohol. It's a condition, not a crime. Maisie, my little sister, is as good as gold – but she's changing too. She used to talk to the whole Gogerty family, her friend Brian, Brian's Mum, Gran, Father Joseph and Kipling, our dog. But since our brother cleared out she's narrowed it down to me, Ma occasionally and Owen – who isn't even here.

Oh, yes, and the latest news is we're dysfunctional! Somebody reported to somebody else that Maisie was being neglected – so we've been sent Miss Blane. She's an old bird with frizzy hair, weird clothes and a fat floppy face full of sickening compassion. She drags on all the time about being a professional – a professional meddler I'd say! She *thinks* she's God's gift. She *thinks* we need her.

Yeah, well, maybe we do – a little. There hasn't been much food around here lately; cooked food I mean. Ma used to make the most luscious things: soda bread and salmon baked in foil, dingle pies and cake . . . she had a way with lemon cake. You could smell it rising in the oven before you got to the gate. It would make us slightly dizzy. We used to run the last bit.

She'd lean against the stove with a glass of wine and a cigarette while we children ate, telling us some outrageous story – laughing. We couldn't resist her laugh. It was . . . God! I've almost forgotten what it was like. No, I haven't; it was catching, it made you lose your head and laugh too – even Owen laughed. Then she'd spread a bit of toast for Maisie and nick one of our sausages with her beautiful long fingers.

Don't get me wrong about Miss Blane, she certainly isn't a cook. But she saw me rooting through Ma's supermarket bags last week and, since then, she makes us tea – not great tea, nothing remotely great about it, but simple things like pancakes and she can do a fair macaroni and cheese.

However, despite the cooking, I'd say Maisie is unlikely to *elect* to talk to Miss Blane. Dead unlikely. Ma can't stand her of course; or rather she can't stand her when she remembers she's here. Mostly she forgets about her existence. Mostly she forgets about ours too.

★   ★   ★

Things are getting worse at home . . . it goes on and on. Yesterday I couldn't help hearing. I was on my way out, but when they're at it my legs don't work. I'd rather have been anywhere else.

"It's deliberate!" Ma was saying. "You're sleeping more, longer nights, longer afternoons, all afternoon . . . It's to get out of being alive. It's to get out of talking to me about him."

Weird! I mean weird stuff. She was prowling round his desk with a glass of red wine in her hand. Dad was just sitting there with his head down. His long curly hair is almost white now and all over the place. The crown of his head looks like a duck's egg. Ma still looks drop-dead gorgeous, fiery and out of control – but gorgeous.

My brother's medical records and a mass of newspaper cuttings were piled on the desk. An X-ray! Why would they want an X-ray? What was that there for? It's horrible! They have them in detective programs when someone's fished out of a river. Owen isn't dead, there's no evidence to say he is.

"You're just shuffling papers, Eddie," she was saying. "Shuffling! It's not real work. You're pretending to work because you think there's nothing more we can do . . ."

Her voice was a climbing scale, the shrill keys you hit with your right hand.

"And you won't keep on looking. You won't keep trying – you can't bear to."

His head sunk lower.

"Coward!" she screamed.

I've heard it all before. Her voice reaches a crescendo then breaks into little bits. Next she starts pleading, begging him to talk to her, going on about her latest theory – concussion, whatever. It's a one-sided battle. I mean Dad doesn't put her down, he doesn't fight back. He just sinks.

I picked up my bag. There's no point in letting it get to you. I have Maisie to think about. I was about to put my earphones on, hating Ma for being so cruel.

Then she said something else. It came out, in a small voice.

"He might be just lying there."

Lying there? Lying where? She's mad – she's totally lost it! But her voice made me want to cry. I mean she *is* my mother. I can't hate her when I love her, can I? I felt like rushing into the room and putting my arms round her . . . but she wouldn't have wanted it to be me.

★   ★   ★

MAISIE

Owen, I was down to the sea with Flo. It was grand! The sky was wide as a dish and the gulls – don't they have a life? They're out after the boats, falling and lifting and calling out one to the other.

There was the salty smell of fish and nets and the lapping, plapping, sighing sounds of little boats..

You've to tell me where gulls go when it gets dark.

I ran an O for you in the wet sand, Owen. Then a big wave came and washed it clean away. It left a mouthful of shells and pebbles where the O had been. Isn't that the way of it?

I'm back at school now and they're writing about me. I saw a big red folder it said **Maisie Grace Gowrie.** *I'm thinking about the Grace in my name. We had it in Scripture class – love given for nothing, is what the teacher said. That's what happens, isn't it? It'll be Jesus put it there.*

They're trying to make me do sounds again at school – Ah's and Fra's and all that. I don't do it. What's the point? I save sounds and words up for Flo. Last night we ran home from the beach shouting them out. The wind caught them and carried them up to the clouds. Then the clouds broke and rain came down and drenched our clothes and sopped our hair. We were laughing all the way up the path. The shells and pebbles jiggled in my pocket.

Miss Blane, Owen, she's a lady not a girl, but she sits with me in class like a girl. What's she after, I wonder? She has a round face and she's plump as a Christmas pullet. At home she's got a bag of wool and stitching patterns and questions for me. I do the sewing and wind the wool and let her pat my hand. 'Maisie!' she says, 'Would you like to use the red thread or the blue thread?' Her lips open in a red shape then a blue shape, as if that would help me to make a word and drop it onto her lap like a sucked sweet. I don't do it, Owen. I don't answer her questions.

One night Ma washed my hair and told me the song of wandering Aengus. She said I was bright as a star. Now which one would that be, I wonder.

I'm off to sleep, now.

I've Grace in my name, Owen, isn't that a marvel?

CHAPTER
2

MISS BLANE

Maisie Gowrie Ref: 001 ASW/RB

I took up my duties with Maisie Gowrie (8), a diagnosed elective mute, one month ago. I pick her up three days a week at eight a.m. I take her to the local primary school, spending the school day with her, encouraging vocal response, integrated play and general participation. I return the child to her home at four p.m. and spend an hour doing the prescribed exercises. At this stage I have made the following observations:

Any communication with teachers and potential playmates is written. As the psychologist Myra Brandt noted, her play is typical of her condition, solitary and repetitive.

Her home situation is far from ideal. The mother drinks. The father is withdrawn. An older sister (15) shows rebellious tendencies and a need for attention.

The health and safety aspects of the home are below standard.

The dysfunctional aspects of Maisie Gowrie's family could be due, in part, to the fact an elder brother went missing in 2010. At this point I have not succeeded in getting Maisie Gowrie to talk to me, although she willingly participates in crafts, games and visual exercises.

Ruth Blane ASW

This short report took time. You've to think what it is they're after with their fancy vocabulary, rules and regulations. It's expected of me of course, but I won't say I'm not pleased with it. I can't help wondering what Mother would say!

"You'll never amount to anything, Toady," was one of her favourite observations. "Either you have it or you don't," was another. "You're just like . . ." but she never would tell me. I never found out who I was just like. "Cheek bones!" she'd say. "The pity of it is you didn't inherit my cheek bones." She was vain about her figure and her bones. When I was little she hit me with a roll of cord or the back of her long scissors if I was late fetching materials. Once, when I dropped the pins, I was locked out of the flat for a whole night. After the accident, when those fine bones of her let her down, she couldn't reach me physically, but it was worse in a way, because I became her full time slave and was hardly ever allowed to go to school. Even then, hunched in her chair like a broken doll, she continued to be vain. "Get me my rouge, Toad," she'd whimper, "and hurry up about it." At other times she'd call me Brat. "You wouldn't understand, Brat deah," she'd say, with sarcastic emphasis on the ah ending of dear, "my side of the family came from good stock. We knew how to dress, instinctively." I dreamt and wondered about the other half, the stock I came from.

Mother was a dressmaker – a good one. After the accident her ladies still came to the flat. She'd direct me from her chair.

hemlines, collars, pleats, I could manage fittings by the age of fourteen. I knew about materials: "two yards of Viyella, and quarter of a yard of duchess satin to cover the buttons for Mrs Thompson's blouse," she'd demand, "and don't forget to pick up my pills." I wanted to please her, but I couldn't. Halfway to the door she'd call me back. "No, Toady, no, you stupid child. Bring me my cushion first, the one for my neck. No! You clumsy creature, move it to the left. You're off like a rocket leaving me without my tea – not that common stuff . . . the Earl Grey, in the tin with the Royal coat of arms, the tea that Lady Sanders left."

Well, I don't have to wonder what Mother would think, do I? If she was alive today I'd have her in a home by now. She'd be slurping PG Tips in a plain cup with no visitors and her rouge out of reach.

There's no doubt that Maisie has taken a liking to me. She lets me comb her hair and hold her hand when we walk to school. When I work with her she's never sulky or rude, just off in her own thoughts. She'll listen to a story well enough or work her samplers, but she'll not talk to me. If she knows I'm in the passage she falls quiet. When she thinks I'm out I hear her voice lifting and falling like a songbird, on about kittens and yellow cake and the red party shoes she loves.

Times are I've a feeling she'd like to tell me something, but it's as if a bit of sacking's stuck in her throat. Of course, as a professional, I know it's not that. Elective mutes have their rules. Places and certain people cause them anxiety. It's in the books. Maisie talks to her mother occasionally, but that mother of hers would cause the Pope anxiety – a hysteric, that's what she is, into the liquor, chasing the shadow of a lad long gone.

The child needs rescuing, that's the sum of it. She needs a normal place with peace and quiet and her glass of milk ready and waiting.

As for Flora Gowrie, now there's trouble! No discipline at all and her clothes . . . flimsy in all weathers with her midriff showing like the section of a snake, an open invitation to the lads. Her tops are like gossamer and her skirts are nothing more than cobbled together handkerchiefs. She's transformed her school uniform and wears the St Ursula's tie knotted round her neck like a gentleman's cravat. Her shoes are a joke on the required footwear and she shows off her ankles to the world with brightly coloured woven strips like a native. You would *not* expect behaviour like that from a St Ursula's girl – it's the smartest private school around. What I say is posh is as posh does – she'd be better off at the local school with Maisie. They wouldn't stand for it.

For all that, she has a good heart and loves her sister. She's a beautiful looking child, not as dark-skinned as her mother, not that foreign untrustworthy skin you can tell came off a boat at some point. Flora's hair is fine and soft like an Irish belle, yet she has a lady's high cheek bones. She has a pretty mouth with the top lip protruding a little, forever on the verge of a laugh or some naughtiness or other. But *her* lips are delicate. While the *mother's* have a pout to them.

Mind you, those two young girls are too skinny by far, they're abandoned and undernourished. It's an outright shame, a case for the courts. Lila Gowrie's idea of shopping is to go to Tesco and idle through the aisles, dropping unsuitable sweets and frozen food into the trolley. Then, I've a suspicion; she stops at Murphy's on the way home for when she gets back she's all over the place like a wild beast, prowling round the house, attacking poor Mr Gowrie, pouring herself another glass of wine from her supply behind the library books, keening for her lost son.

The bags get dumped in the pantry and the girls root through them like foxes. They'll pick out a box of biscuits and share them then and there on the floor, leaving a mess of crumbs behind.

Well, that's where I come in. I've compassion, you see, I can do my work and know when the moment has come to go outside my job description.

"Get up off that floor!" I said to Flora the other day. "I'll get your tea!"

"You'll get our tea?" she shot back at me. "What's it to be then, bread, followed by bread and butter?"

She's a cheek on her you'd not believe, no wonder her teachers are at their wit's end. But I started sorting and before long I'd a meal on the table.

And that's not what it sounds, not at all! To get to the kitchen you've to walk down a long passage past old saddles and bridles through a room full of wellingtons that must go back fifty years. You've to pass through another room with an enormous table they call the ironing room. For the love of God, you'd need to be a giant to iron on that table! The kitchen is out of the ark. The stove is one of those old-fashioned ones that wants a bucket of coal and a riddle of an evening. The kettle weighs a ton and the fridge is in a shed outside the back door surrounded by nettles.

I haven't counted the cats, but they're all over the place, flattening themselves out on the ironing and licking cream out a jug if they've half a chance. Then there's Donnie, an ancient servant, who turns up now and then to puff his pipe in the rocking chair and waste everyone's time. Like Marion the donkey, he's too old to work, but not too old to need spoiling the life out of.

In the papers they're always on about Cleary Court: a Georgian treasure, a magnificent example of this and that. What I have to say is those fancy architects should take a closer look. It does have grandeur I will say, and I've a natural taste for grandeur!

But, open your eyes and you'll see wallpaper curling off the wall like a bunch of celery. And, imagine this, there's a patch where rain drips through the ceiling – they take turns emptying the bucket, as if it were the most natural thing in the world.

Still, for all that, I took pity on the children and got the oven going and made them a fine meal. Before long Mr Gowrie crept in and took his place at the table. He's a lovely man, half-starved if you ask me, but mannerly; shy and mannerly.

★ ★ ★

I'm shaking this morning, shaking from head to toe. Last night a scene took place in the Gowrie household like in one of those soap operas over from America.

Mr Breen, the Gowrie's family lawyer, had some news to impart regarding their son. We were to assemble in the drawing room at six o'clock and he wished me to be included. He's a respectable gentleman with letters after his name. He arrived punctually in a Vauxhall wearing a chalk-striped suit with a bit of a shine to it, and a fine yellow tie.

When I came in with Maisie the mood in the room wasn't right, not right at all. There'd been a turn in the weather. It was close; a heavy sky, yet not a drop of rain. I could tell Lila Gowrie had been drinking. She was dressed to kill in a cream-coloured silk blouse with a tight, black skirt, showing off those fine legs of hers. She was keyed up like a horse before a race, skittery yet tense with hope.

Mr Gowrie sat at his desk arranging his papers. I noticed he'd a slight sweat on his brow. Nonetheless, he had time for a 'good evening' to me and a smile for Maisie, which is more than can be said for *her*. My heart goes out to the man.

We'd to wait for Flora who came in late, nodding her head to music the rest of us couldn't hear. Maisie brought her sketch book, she lay down on her stomach and began to colour a night sky. She never looked up, but you could tell the child was upset; When voices were raised she drew faster, the tips of her colours breaking, planets and stars colliding on the page.

"Well, Mr Breen," Lila Gowrie said, taking centre stage. "It's wonderful news! We hear you've turned up something at last. You have a lead . . . regarding our son?"

"At this stage it's very tentative, Mrs Gowrie," he replied. "I must ask you not to get excited. There is information which we need to go over. I would like to include your daughters and the social worker in this session."

"I'm afraid that won't do you much good. Flora is not exactly reliable," Lila Gowrie said with a confidential smile and a disparaging nod at the earphones. The girl took them off with a rude shrug. "And I'm sorry to say our youngest daughter has a slight impediment, Mr Breen – she doesn't speak. As for Miss Brain here; Oh, I'm sorry! I mean Miss Blane . . . well, she didn't even know him, so you're stuck with us," she laughed lightly, "but we'll do our best."

"Nonetheless . . ." he started off.

"A whiskey, Mr Breen?" Her voice was high-pitched and manically positive, as if she could manufacture success by thrusting the gentleman into a corner. It was plain to see he was not to be thrusted. You couldn't fault his demeanour.

"No thank you, Mrs Gowrie."

She walked seductively over to him all the same, putting an unasked for whiskey on the table beside him.

"Eddie! Tell him to start, for God's sake."

"Lila dear, give the man a chance."

The lawyer explained that he was taking a new approach to their son's disappearance, looking at it from the point of view of trauma in the boy's childhood and certain aspects of his character. He'd been working with child psychologists rather than the police.

This seemed to go down well with the family. He started by asking Mr Gowrie if he would describe his son as particularly sensitive to the suffering of others, an impulsive young person who wished to save the world?

"I would describe him as concerned." Mr Gowrie replied. "Wouldn't you agree, Flora?"

"Well, yeah . . . he liked people, if that's abnormal? He didn't do any saving here, but he changed a bit at Uni."

"Ah-ha, changed! In what way?" The lawyer asked, switching his attention to her.

"Now let me see, Mr Breen, would a T-shirt that said *Peace* be evidence of a world-saver? And what about poetry? He'd a great love for poetry and, on various occasions, he's been seen with poets . . ."

There was the trace of a smile on the father's face. The mother looked daggers.

"Stop it, Flo!" Lila Gowrie shouted, "*Dios mio*! You idiotic child. Let's hear what our lawyer has to say." She topped up her glass in full view of anyone who cared to look. "Do *please* go on, Mr Breen."

The lawyer asked Mr Gowrie why he'd used the word *concerned*.

"Simply because my son, our son, had an unusually tender," he paused, "compassion, you could call it, for the . . ." For a minute he appeared to stop talking. His colour was high, his hands shook. "For the troubled – the dispossessed," he went on slowly. "He planned to go abroad, after he had finished his studies."

The lawyer looked pleased. "Might his impatience to help the dispossessed have advanced his plans to go abroad?"

"It is possible," Mr Gowrie said cautiously.

"Possible and probable!" Mr Breen said triumphantly. Then, out of the blue, he brought up the subject of the Haiti earthquake. He began to describe the cholera and the chaos that's still going on. The Gowrie family looked puzzled. Lila Gowrie didn't let the gentleman get far . . .

"Could we *please* stick to the point, dear Mr Breen?" She flashed him one of her artificial smiles. "Our son," she reminded him. "You said you had uncovered some intelligence? We were so hoping for intelligence, weren't we Eddie?"

Then Flora was up on her feet, butting in as usual. "You see we know about Haiti, Mr B, everyone does. It's awful! They're like *us*, don't you see? Just like us, not knowing where their people are."

The lawyer told her firmly that the people in Haiti were *not* just like us, not at all. It was important that she understood that Haiti is a third world country – and a very poor one at that.

"So?" Flora challenged him. "So, not really worth worrying about, Mr Breen? I mean what's ten million poor people, really . . . in a country that doesn't have oil?"

"Flora!" Her father was angry. "One more remark like that and you'll leave the room."

Passions were rising. The room was hot. The fire spat a chip of burning coal onto the rug, then another. I was up in a flash stamping them out. I tried to open the big bay window, but it was jammed. Outside a roll of thunder unravelled across the fields, like a heavy ball of wool that won't be stopped.

"I apologise for my daughter," Mrs Gowrie said insincerely, "but do explain what on earth Haiti has to do with us, Mr Breen? Aren't we spinning off on one of your little tangents? I wouldn't care a hoot if my son was out there. I'd be proud."

The lawyer was not to be put down. He took an initialled

handkerchief out of his pocket and polished his glasses. He faced his adversary head on. I had to remind myself that I wasn't watching television. It was a first class performance.

"Indeed, Mrs Gowrie, I'm sure you would be proud. But I suspect you might mind a hoot if he has been caught up in the ensuing chaos. Are you aware that our embassy has specifically warned volunteers against going out there? Are you aware of the crime: the looting, armed robberies, kidnapping and murder that is taking place? I have it all here. I suggest that you will be very upset indeed if your son is among the young people who have chosen to ignore the warnings."

Mr Gowrie looked Mr Breen straight in the eye and asked him if he had indications that their son was in Haiti.

Mr Breen didn't pause. He was in full flow asking us to imagine the scene: collapsed houses, cholera, bodies, sewage, contaminated drinking water . . . hundreds of thousands dead. Had they never heard of an Irishman called Donovan? Had they heard of Rapid Response? This man was managing a water distribution project there. He knew many of the kids who had swamped into Haiti. He had descriptions of the ones that had come to grief. Mr Donovan, didn't know Owen but he bewailed the fact that this tragedy had attracted foolish, untrained young people who, like their son . . .

"Like our son?" Lila broke in. "From abroad? Did you say children from abroad?"

"I did, Mrs Gowrie."

Flora was quiet for once, gazing at her mother. Lila touched the pearls at her throat with nervous fingers.

"Mrs Gowrie, I am here to tell you that a team of British forensic specialists has been sent . . ."

"What did you say?" Lila Gowrie levelled the words at the lawyer, slowly, steadily, like pistol shots.

"Forensic spec . . ."

She stood straight and tall, not an easy thing with all that liquor inside her, but she stood like a queen facing her lowliest subject. Mr Breen looked fearful. He took a step back.

"You," she paused, letting the word soak in scorn, "you said you had something to tell us, something helpful, something concerning our son. How dare you come to this house and mention death? How dare you use that *palabra espantosa* – forensic?"

"Lila!" her husband cried out. He left his desk and started towards her.

"You," Lila Gowrie screamed at Mr. Breen, springing at him like a panther, "were employed to look for a living son, not . . ."

"No, Ma, no!" Flora wailed. She grabbed her sister and covered her eyes. Maisie whimpered.

It was clear as daylight she wasn't going to make it. Her glass flew from her hand and shattered round the man's patent leather shoes. Then she fell, crashed to the ground right there in front of her husband and daughters.

★ ★ ★

What to do in a crisis, that was part of it, part of the training. I kept my head. I was there in a minute, picking her up carefully but firmly. She was light in my arms, gone from powerful to frail in seconds.

"Not dead, not a dead son," she kept repeating, as I got her up the stairs and into her room. She was out for the count by the time I laid her down.

I straightened up and caught my breath. I'd never been in Lila Gowrie's bedroom before. It wasn't picked up and neat, but I've never seen a lovelier room. The linen was cream and finely worked, and there were touches of rose where embroidered cushions were tossed on top of the pillows. Her dressing table had little bottles with antique silver tops and there was a padded jewellery box with the lid off – pearls, moonstones and silver all in a jumble. A glint caught my eye. A ruby and diamond ring was fallen, lying on the carpet. I knew better than to touch it.

The curtains were white too, edged with wild flowers. The window was open. It was raining heavily now and the wind was up, filling the curtains like a sail with dark night air.

I looked back at her. I should finish the job, no doubt about it. There was a silk slip hanging over a chair – that would be her nightgown. I wasn't afraid. What was she, after all? An out and out drunk, nothing more, nothing less. I lifted her thighs roughly, and got her skirt off. Then I undid her blouse and bra and pulled them off too. But when I laid her back down again I saw there was a cut on her arm and one of her breasts was smeared with blood.

It was my duty to wash her, but I faltered. I think it was the room affected my senses. This naked woman, vulnerable on the bed, and the flying white curtains – or maybe it was the scent coming off her, a foreign smell, light but intoxicating. I gathered myself together and fetched a basin of warm water and a sponge and set about the task. But this time I found myself gentle. Poor creature! The state she was in. I didn't look at her body, mind, but her body was – beautiful. I shut my eyes when I put on the slip. and stroked it down the length of her. You don't want runkles, do you? You want it lying smooth, so that's what I did. I was the professional, washing a patient like a nurse in a hospital.

It was far too late for me to be going home. I looked in on Maisie, but her bed was empty. I found the sisters sleeping together in Flora's room.

I went downstairs to check the house. The lights were all on and the hall window flapping with rain pouring in. I was round the place in no time, closing and snibbing. The front door was blown wide open. I shut it. They don't lock the door here, that was one of the first things I was told: "Never!" she'd said to me in her autocratic way, "lock the front door. Is that fully understood?" It's tragic when you think about it. Do they really imagine that lad of theirs will come slinking home in the night like a wet collie?

I thought Edward Gowrie would've gone to bed forgetting to shut up, but when I got to the library there he was at his desk, staring ahead of him. I was creeping past, making for the stairs, when I thought to go back, for I'd never seen such a lonesome creature. The wreckage was still all over the floor, the upturned chair, the broken glass and a puddle of spilled whiskey.

I think he saw me, but like a sleeping man.

"Mr Gowrie?" I said.

"Mr. Gowrie! The house is shut up now. The girls are in bed."

He didn't stir.

"It's time to go upstairs now."

I don't know men; I've not had a thing to do with a grown man, but I'd a sense of it last night. I put out my hand. After a while he took it and let me lead him upstairs. He lay down obediently by his wife. I took off his shoes, that was all, more than enough. The room was closing in on me again, cloudy with their intimacy

*   *   *

As I was going to sleep in their fine monogrammed linen sheets, it occurred to me that I'd gone outside my job description – way outside and beyond what was required of me.

FLORA

Ma went flying right over the top last night. I mean literally *flying* – it was crazy. I wanted to hold her; I wanted to lie on top of her to protect her from that creep Breen and Miss B touching her with her fat fingers. Yuk! I'm not being gross but her arm was bleeding and her blouse was undone. This thing happens when she's been drinking – her mouth is awry, like a cartoon. I hated them seeing her like that. I wanted to go to her, but when I saw it coming I covered Maisie's eyes with my hands and held her close.

She did it in style this time. That fool of a lawyer used one of the forbidden words – *forensic*. That did it! She went for him. But somehow she lost her balance and crashed to the ground. Dad started to go to her, but then he gave way to Miss Blane who took over, fussing and flapping and jerking Ma to her feet. I couldn't bear Maisie seeing any of it. Somehow I got her upstairs to my room.

'Maisie, daisy, give me your answer do.
I'm half crazy, all for the love of you . . .'

I put her nightie over her head and kissed her toes and did the things she likes when she's scared. By the time I got to

And you'll look sweet, upon the seat
Of a bicycle made for two.'

she was sitting up, listening.
"Where's Ma, Flo?" she asked.

"Sleeping, Maisie – did you not notice how tired she was?"

"Where's Dad?"

"He'll be putting the guard round the fire like always, and shutting up." She sighed.

"Owen doesn't like a lot of noise, does he, Flo?"

"No, he does not."

"He'll be glad he wasn't in tonight, then?"

"Yes."

"Mr Breen's as blind as a mole. Isn't that right, Flo?"

"You've said it!"

"If Owen were right beside him he'd never know it, like in the Jesus stories."

"Blind as a mole." I agreed.

She smiled and lay down with Moll doll in her arms. Maisie often identifies Owen with Jesus.

I don't agree about my brother having the remotest resemblance to Jesus. For all his peaceful philosophy he set off a time bomb in this family when he left. It's ticking every day as we all go madder. It's a luxury just walking out, leaving the people who love you not knowing. Not knowing is worse than dead. At least being dead is normal – a wake, masses said, a body to bury, a stone to prove the body's there, a name on the stone. OK, it's sad. But at least it's normal.

There are millions of dead people here; they are settled amongst the cypress trees above the estuary where the wild flowers are. Their families aren't like ours. They have photographs of the person on the mantelpiece. "That's Georgie fishing when he was ten," they say with a wistful smile, "and here he is at the Dublin Horse Show in 1985." They can cry, or laugh. They're free to faint over the grave if they want to, or throw themselves in – whatever.

My mother won't allow herself to think there's reason to cry. She's not about to. She's expecting Owen back.

★　★　★

What none of them know is what happened the summer I was thirteen. That bummer Breen couldn't get it out of me if he prised me apart with a chisel. It's almost a clue, now I think about it, the tall man in a suit and the blonde woman who were staying in the upper rooms at O'Flanigan's. They weren't from around here. The woman had a glossy look – white flared trousers and shiny pink shoes with kitten heels. *Not*, absolutely not, what you'd find in Cork.

That summer I was into spying on Owen. He would slip away and hang out with them. They had covered books, like the ones in primary schools – one each – and masses of papers. Sometimes they'd pore over them, at other times they'd sit in the pub garden in silence.

Another thing! The woman was a lady, not a girl. Really old, maybe twenty-five, or more. Anyway, one evening it was just her and Owen alone. I followed them. They took the sea path above Ballygore Bay and stopped and kissed. Then they cut in a bit and lay down in the wild thyme.

I mean, I saw it happen! My brother doing it with this woman. I was lying on my stomach behind a rock and she was moaning so you could hear it above the gulls. They rolled over and over. Owen's back was scratched with her long, pearly fingernails. It was better than a PG movie.

I thought sex was the secret then, but now I think it's more about those strangers at the pub. They were after Owen, no doubt about it.

They could have been Mafia – but the clothes weren't right. And the blonde woman didn't look like a Mafia bitch, not really. Maybe they wanted him for a mission, passing something on to somebody?

Or a killing? But he'd be useless at that. Or perhaps they had something on him, something we don't know about.

Whatever, it was so strong that it took hold of my brother, wrapped itself round his heart and moved him to leave us, without a word, without a note. Even people who commit suicide leave notes.

I told Owen I'd seen him up there. He made me promise not to tell, ever. I liked that. I love secrets. You could say he was my hero then, so I kept my promise. I should have told Ma and Dad, I realize that now. But, if I'd told them about the pub and the books and the woman, I'd have had to tell them about the sex – and that's one thing you so don't talk to parents about. I mean, forget it!

In one of Breen's private inquisitions he asked me if I remembered how and when Owen left home. For once I told him the truth: 'No, nothing! I remember nothing about it, no empty chair at dinner, no backpack bumping downstairs in the middle of the night.'

But now when I try hard to remember it seems that it was gradual, like a storm gathering over the sea, bigger waves, then a flat sky empty of birds – eventually even the jetty disappears.

At the end of September he didn't turn up at university. That was when it got real. The police were at our house all the time. There were questions flying, photographers, recorded interviews and doors closed in our faces. They found out he'd missed lectures the term before and he'd left the flat he was sharing ages before that. There was a rumour that he'd been living in Belfast for a while, sleeping rough, but it turned out it was a different Owen who played an electric guitar.

The police came up with the unoriginal idea that he must be doing drugs. Mad! I mean masses of people are into drugs, it's what parents expect – I could have told them you don't have to disappear for that. In any case Owen doesn't like putting foreign substances into his body. He doesn't drink coffee. He likes wine, not spirits. I'd say that's a relevant detail.

It's odd because Maisie and I still didn't take it in. I didn't believe it was possible – it seemed like the script for a film that wouldn't be taken on. As for Maisie, she's never believed he's gone, still doesn't. For her dogs and people she loves never leave.

We went on with our lives. But gradually Ma began to change. Darts of fear, in little liquid spurts, began to criss-cross her eyes. She stiffened, muscle by muscle. Her face closed like an envelope. The words we were used to hearing, her questions, games, jokes and scolding began to disintegrate. Dad was strong then, handling everything, confident in the police, taking on Breen, making sure that Maisie and I had proper meals . . .

But that Christmas Owen didn't come home and at last it sunk in. With an electric jolt I realized he had gone, really gone. And immediately I wanted him back; desperately, urgently, frantically wanted him back . . .

It was like leaking gas, the space he left behind. His absence filled our house. His voice was and wasn't everywhere, in every room. I mean, when you know what a person will say and how they'll say it and suddenly that voice isn't there, you still hear it, of course you do. It can't be stopped. And when you're used to a person's laugh and something silly happens – the sort of thing you both think is funny – you wait for it, but the laugh doesn't come. And in the morning, some mornings that is, you wake up and forget it's happened. You run downstairs, you might need the person to do something, you might be cross with him, or happy. But then you remember he's gone. He isn't going to be in the kitchen – or anywhere else for that matter.

★   ★   ★

I've made up my mind. I'm going to get Owen back for Ma and Dad and Maisie. I'll wait till my sixteenth birthday, then I'll go. For one thing I'll be able to ask for money. For another, sixteen is easy for parents to take. Totally normal! A grown-up daughter leaving home? It's no big deal.

I won't tell them where I am, but I will tell them I've gone to find him. I'll ring to let them know I'm OK. I'm not going for the *missing* act like my brother. I *so* wouldn't put them through that. I mean, no way. And why would they worry? That's the thing . . . I'm not into sex. It's unoriginal and frankly the boys in Ballymore are not a turn on. They're there for the taking, slouching around copying each other. Mostly they're into computer games and when they make a grab you have to take on board you're just another game – like you are one of their oriental victims, supposed to burst into blue flames when they make a hit. Who needs it?

I'm not against it – sex, that is. And I'm certainly not saving myself for some born-again bloke saving himself for a good girl who is saving herself for a good guy who is actually an uncool, clean-shaven, closet-computer-game-playing creep. No! I'm just not on for it. And I'm not into drugs except for natural stuff, like pot and magic mushrooms, only I haven't found any mushrooms yet.

I'll tell Maisie. She'll be glad I've gone to get Owen. She's expecting him, anyway. She's been expecting him for over a year. But who will take care of her? She'll be . . . without me. Ma loves her passionately, but she forgets things like supper and getting to school on time, or getting to school at all. She can't help it. It's alcohol – and sorrow. And poor Dad, his eyes droop, you have to wake him up for a game of dominoes.

Thing is, Maisie won't be alone, not anymore, because *she's* here . . . Blane! It's weird, but that frumpy old, bossy old creature adores her. She makes excuses to spend the night, 'though she's not supposed to. She folds Maisie's nightie, like *tenderly*, and lets her take the kittens upstairs. Look! I've seen her break into a heavy skip just to make my sister smile and, when Maisie eats her chicken pie, her eyes go blurry, like rained-on glass. It's odd, but she's verging on sweet with little M.

Maisie will be cool with it – I'm sure she will . . .

MAISIE

Owen, you'd not have believed it! Mr Breen was up to the house again. We were in the library – all together. It wasn't a party, although Ma was dressed up, pretty as pretty, giving the man a nice drink to himself. But Mr Breen wasn't smiling. He started in asking questions like a teacher and Dad was answering them like a boy. The questions made him sad.

He had come to tell us about you and he doesn't even know you! Wasn't that the nonsense of it? The room was full of voices, all coming out at the same time like bubbles in a kettle. You wouldn't have liked Mr Breen's voice. It was kept down, like a dog on a tight lead. You could hear a shout hidden there, although it was never let go.

For certain you wouldn't have liked the noise, Owen. You don't have a shout in you.

Mr Breen's words trundled over my head. There was time to colour in three skies. The talking went on and on. There was a storm coming our way – Miss Blane tried to open the window but it was stuck. It got hotter and hotter.

Then suddenly there was a cry and a sharp tinkling of glass, and Dad's frightened voice and falling, the sound of something falling. A moan was coming out of my mouth, like it did on the day Kipling died. I couldn't see what happened for Flo's hands were covering my eyes.

Then Flo was up the stairs with me in her arms, for all that I'm four and a half stone. It's the first time I've been carried since the time you brought me home from Mallow Fair. Flo sang Maisie Daisy to me. The tune is fast inside my head.

In the morning I was dressed and ready to see Ma, but Flo told me she was tired out and we should leave her be – so we went downstairs and ate our porridge like always. And today it's Saturday.

But something fell. I couldn't tell what it was. Now the falling sound is in my head with the Maisie Daisy tune. It was more of a thud than a break, more of a bump than a crash. A cry circled in the air beating its wings like a frightened bird.

CHAPTER
3

MISS BLANE

On a good evening he'll go down to the marsh. "Transatlantic waders," he tells me, "you may see a buff-breasted sandpiper or whimbrels if you're lucky." He says this shyly, glancing up at me, glad to have someone asking bird questions. Sure and I don't know a duck from a dove myself, but I love to hear him talk. "Nice!" I say to encourage him. 'It must be nice out there in the bog.' 'Nice?' he repeats, as if I were talking in a foreign tongue. "Yes, I suppose it is . . . yes, indeed."

He sets off in his baggy corduroy trousers with his binoculars banging against his torn jacket. He's forgotten his boots again. His trousers are soaked in the long grass before he's reached the wall, but he's over it no trouble at all. Although his hair is ribbed grey and white he has a fine body, not an old man's body, I'd put him at about sixty-seven – or maybe sixty-five. It's just his face that's aged, what with having such a harridan for a wife and that boy of his taking off. There's not a thing wrong with him that a haircut and a little loving kindness wouldn't cure.

The household is back to normal now, as normal as it gets, that is. Lila Gowrie stayed in her room for two days after the night Mr Breen was here. Flora was up and down those stairs with trays and flowers for her mother, but now Mrs G's returned to the land of the living, drinking herself silly again, as bad as ever she was.

★ ★ ★

Father Joseph was over for his tea the other day. You'll not get a more respected priest in Cork – or out of it for that matter. You won't hear a bad word said about him.

Lila Gowrie is an exhibitionist Catholic if ever I saw one! She trips into mass dressed in her Armani suit with her hair piled up on her head and a small veiled hat to top it off. The suit is a dark grey stripe and fits her well. She doesn't deserve a figure like that at her age.

She causes a stir alright and, if you ask me, a stir is what she's after. When she makes her way up to the front pew, you can hear the whispers . . .

"Will you look at her, poor thing, with her lad still gone."

"He'll have passed on by now, for certain sure."

"She didn't buy that outfit in Cork, I'm telling you!"

"Sure and she's hardly put up a pound since then."

Father Joseph has to hush them to get their noses back in their prayer books.

It's hard to say if Lila Gowrie loves Father Joseph or not. Sometimes he can do no wrong, other days he gets it in the neck like the rest of us. Yesterday Flora and I were present at a heated discussion right there at the tea table. The priest came over to suggest a mass for the intentions of her son. Flora told me later they'd been through it all before and her mother didn't want a mass said for her son because he wasn't dead.

Father Joseph is small. He stands on a block in the pulpit. When you can't see the block he's as impressive as you could wish for, but in real life he's the height of a ten-year-old. When

Lila Gowrie greeted him he was wearing a plain navy suit and a dog collar. He stood on the points of his slippers like a ballet dancer, determined to hold his own.

She'd baked a toffee cake for the occasion. (I will say she has a knack with a cake when she puts her mind to it) It's feast or famine for those girls.

At first there were the pleasantries. 'Father do you think this . . . ? Father would you agree that . . . ?' We sat down for tea, but the minute he introduced the subject of a mass she was off:

"It's out of the question, Father. *Prohibido!*" she said, raising her voice.

"And what would you be meaning by that?" he asked."

"Do you want it in Latin – *prohibitum est?* Or would Greek suit you better, Father?"

"Now Mrs Gowrie, I don't tink you fully understand t'nature of a mass for the intentions of a missing person. It's appropriate after all this time. It's not like a mass for the dead, not at all, at all. It's a joyful thing, indeed it is, a fine way of showing our faith in young Owen and wishing him well wherever . . ."

"Listen to him, Ma!" Flora begged. "Give him a . . ."

"My son is not a corpse or a cripple, Father Joseph," she interrupted. "I know all there is to know about masses, I could outmass you any day of the week. Besides, you are missing an adjective."

"And what might that be?"

"Good! My son's intentions were always good, Father. They still are. Ask anyone."

At this point Father Joseph got to his feet to better take on his adversary. It was a mistake, for even on tiptoes, even with little jumps here and there, he looked small, a lot smaller than she is. She sat elegantly sipping her tea, with a superior look on her face, as he delivered his lecture.

"You've a sharp tongue on you, Mrs Gowrie, and a keen nose for a quarrel (*jump.*) D'you not remember only the other day you were asking me up here to read the beatitudes with you? (*smaller jump*). It's a hard thing for me to have to remind yourself (*he almost lost his balance but caught the table in time and sat down panting*) but weren't we after reciting the sacred text together: *Blessed are the meek for they . . .*"

"You're getting confused, Father Joseph, between my son and me. My son *is* meek in spirit and he *will* be comforted if he wants. If it's a sinner you're looking for, you have one right here."

"Then I'll be seeing you at confession this very Sunday?" the priest rapped back at her.

"Oh, I wouldn't want to take up so much of your time, Father Joseph!"

She thought it was a fine joke but the little man was exhausted, mopping his face and shaking his head mournfully. "Take good care of your mother, there's a good girl," he said to Flora as she showed him out. And she promised him she would, meek as a lamb herself, for once in her life.

You never know what you're in for in this house. Did I say 'back to normal?' I must be losing my mind.

★   ★   ★

After two months with the Gowrie family my next report was due. I'd been looking forward to a professional update, going into my progress with Maisie, relaying the latest information regarding the family situation, writing as an experienced Assistant Social Worker – in line for promotion, I don't doubt. The first part was simple enough:

I have established a satisfactory rhythm in my work with Maisie Gowrie, following the tasks identified at our initial

51

planning meeting. I went on, repeating the daily ritual with ease, but then I hesitated. The next section was headed **PROGRESS**. There has not been any progress to speak of and the school is well aware of it. The authorities in my profession set great store by progress. I realized that a certain delicacy in my language would be necessary, little adjustments here and there. I paused and cast my eyes down to the next column. **HOME SITUATION**. I looked back at my first report and felt uncomfortable. Supposing they were to take Maisie into care? Why, it would kill Edward and Flora and, the truth of it was, for all her neglect I had to admit it would drive Lila Gowrie right off her head, for when she does notice her children there's a sort of love-violence in it, like all her other violences.

Only the other night I was about to wash Maisie's hair. I took the liberty. The child doesn't much like being touched, but I've a way with her and its over and done with in no time. I don't want them thinking she isn't cared for at the school, do I? Well I was taking her upstairs when I heard her mother's voice . . .

"Where do you think you're going?"

I told her Maisie's hair was dirty and I was happy to help out. But she had to interfere. She held out her arms to the child who ran right to her.

"Would it be fun for me to wash your hair in my bathroom, darling?" she said. "No fingers – just the big blue comb that doesn't tug."

She stroked her daughter's hair, twirling it round her hand, winding it into a chignon, looking at me defiantly.

"Or would you like *her* to do it in the nursery bathroom?"

Of course Maisie was off without a backward glance. That's what I've to put up with, after all my work.

With Flora it's the same. I've seen them lying on the sofa like schoolgirls reading poems out loud and, even when they fight, something mysterious binds them together. There was a row to blow the roof off the other day. Like all her lot Flora Gowrie's forever on her fancy telephone. "Any response from over there?" her mother remarked the other day. She was busy preparing mayonnaise the hard way with an old-fashioned whisk. 'Just talking to a friend,' the girl replied. "Ah! Would that be a human friend or an electronic one?" "What do you care?" Flora replied, tapping on without looking up. "Oh, I don't!" Lila Gowrie said, "I'm getting used to having a live-in Martian as a daughter." Flora stared at her for a moment then snapped back: 'Like Maisie and I are getting used to having a live-in lush for a mother?'

They were on fire, just like that, glaring at each other over the bowl of mayonnaise. "How dare you, you little . . ." "Go on, Mother, say it. Say it! Swear at me, like you swear at poor Dad." Flora's eyes filled with tears. Her mother stormed out of the room.

But when I tried to comfort the girl I got it in the neck. "You keep out of it, Miss B! You don't know a thing about my mother. She's noble. She has Latin blood. She studied music at the National Conservatory. Her family stood up against Franco, her father was the top history professor in Madrid University before he was beaten up by the Civil Guard – the whole family had to flee to England. You wouldn't know the first thing about it. You don't know *shite*."

The child is sobbing and shakes me off when I try to put my arm round her.

Sure and I'm not daft. I can tell the mother is posh, but it's foreign posh and that counts for nothing in my book. If it's posh you're looking for give me a man like Edward Gowrie. He's got Anglo- Irish blood and Cambridge behind him. There's pictures of him in teams in the downstairs lavatory.

I looked back at the form. I had to mind my language. If they took Maisie away it would finish us all off.

PROGRESS: I am happy to report that, due to my efforts in this department, Maisie Gowrie's speech is now fluent in the home environment. I have reason to anticipate that this improvement will soon be reflected in her school life.

I liked my phraseology. I liked the fact that except for the small omission that it was not to me that she spoke fluently it was almost true. After this, my text flowed freely. The word dysfunctional had to be blotted out from their memories.

HOME SITUATION Familiarity with the Gowrie family has led me to believe that my first impression was mistaken; they form a close family unit, supportive of each other and young Maisie. I found myself describing Lila as a merry, vibrant character and Edward Gowrie as a dignified man who took his parenting duties seriously. Flora, I told them, was a typical teenager, fond of music and clothes. Their question about the effects on the family of having a missing son made me angry. God knows, I'm sick to death of hearing about their famous son! The effects on the family of having a missing son are much exaggerated by the press and society at large, I wrote. This wholesome family has come to terms with its situation and is moving on. Ruth Blane ASW

I speak their language, you see! It's professional idiom, familiar to a person of my standing. What they don't know is that Maisie is almost mine now, the child I never had. Surges! I feel surges through the length of me. It's mother love, I can tell. It's the nurturing instinct. Far be it from me to infer what's best left alone, but a blind man can see that Lila Gowrie is not long for this world. She must have a liver like a bog under that superficial beauty.

And if something were to happen to her . . . ? Why then, I'd be here, wouldn't I? I'd be the one to step right into her shoes.

A letter was waiting for me when I got back to the flat the following Friday. I made myself a cup of tea, shook off my shoes, squeezed out of my figure-forming knickers and opened it. 'Mother of God!' I said out loud. It was a message from Eileen O'Hanson who took the course with me. I call her my friend, but she's the type who'll have you laughing your head off one minute then, as soon as you're out of sight, you'll be fodder for her next story. All the same she's an assistant teacher at Maisie's school and has a keen ear for gossip, so I read it carefully, two times through.

She wrote that she'd overheard talk in the staff room. Apparently Mrs Gowrie had insulted a mother whose child had given Maisie a push in the playground. The woman had defended herself which caused Lila to give *her* a push to show what it felt like. Both pushes were reported to Mrs Scott, the headmistress.

There was worse to come. Eileen O'Hanson had overheard rumours of unsettling psychological behaviour in my past concerning the remains of a wheelchair washed up on the beach. Imagine that! If they'd taken the trouble to find out what was in that chair the death of a dressing gown is all they'd have come up with. Two *concerned adults* were going to drop by on Tuesday afternoon to reassure themselves all was well in the Gowrie household. It was to be a surprise visit, supposedly to observe Maisie in her home setting.

The bastards, I thought. Don't I know all about their observation tactics? Their eyes'll be all over the place, sniping into corners. They'll have discreet little pads on their knees with a column for me: *Is Ruth Blane keeping the right professional balance? Her relationship with Maisie? Her relationship with other members of the family? Mrs Gowrie's mothering skills . . .*

And the hour. . . Lila's at her worst when she comes down from her rest, they'll smell the liquor on her breath. My job! They'll have my job off me, I thought. It was a Friday evening. I'd no reason to go back to the house till Monday. I had to warn them, but who would heed me?

It came upon me then, clear as day that – I'll not use the word *love* for a job – but the truth is I've made my place at Cleary Court. It's where I'm needed with little Maisie and the rest. I like being where I can keep an eye on Edward Gowrie, seeing he gets a bit of breakfast in him, helping him to find his spectacles. I'd been hoping to stay over nights now and then . . . just a private arrangement, of course.

I hate this flat. The damp gets to my bones. I trudge up the steps, grapple with the key and the first thing I see is Mother's dummy. She is one of the old-fashioned ones, sitting on a lead base. She's here waiting for me every evening – headless, with swollen cloth bosoms and no nipples. She brings it all back, puts me right off my tea. I hear Mother's whine: 'Bra-aat? Is that you?' I smell her smell. I feel the dig of her fingers where she grasped me when I lifted her onto the toilet.

That dummy was always on her side. Smug! Smug as you can be without a head. She'd be draped in a skirt that needed hemming, or half a sleeve that was wanting a puff. I'd have that dummy over the cliff too by now, if I'd the strength to budge her.

I put my mind to saving my job. It would never do to talk to Mr Gowrie. He's a man forlorn, retired from conflict, worn out with it. Flora wouldn't want Maisie taken away, she'd fight for her like a wildcat, but she's a child herself and has the teachers' backs up at school, for all her cleverness. The more I thought about it the more I realized I'd have to walk right into the enemy's camp if I wanted help – only *she* has the power.

⋆　⋆　⋆

The next morning I went to Cleary Court. A briar rose was out, not trained at all, but a lovely sight for all that. There wasn't a sign of the family, but then I heard music. That'd be her up in the old nursery where she has her grand piano in amongst school trunks, and the rocking horse that Maisie loves. I climbed the narrow stairs and stood in the doorway watching her.

It wasn't the sort of thing you could interrupt. I like an Irish song with a lilt to it myself, but she was absorbed in some classical piece, bending over the keys, stroking them. Her bare feet sank and rose from the pedals, moving the sound from a painful ache to softer, sweeter strains. There was beauty in it, I'm bound to say. She was wearing a short silk dressing-gown tied round her waist with a bit of rope. Suddenly she stopped and looked round, surprised.

"What on *earth* are you doing here? Isn't this Saturday?" Her voice was cool, not exactly unkind.

"It's kind of an emergency, Mrs Gowrie," I said. They're coming to check on us."

"Who is?"

"A representative from Maisie's school and a psychologist."

"Why? What's wrong with Maisie?"

"Mrs Gowrie, it's not just . . ."

"Lila, for God's sake! Call me Lila and come to the point."

"It's not just Maisie, Lila."

"Oh?"

"No, but she's the one that'll suffer. It's this house, and not having normal food and the neglect. It's not caring for the girls right . . . They'll take her into care, they'll bring down destruction on us all."

She swung round on her piano stool to face me and took a

cigarette out of her pocket. She was smiling now, not taking me seriously. One hand strayed back to the piano and played a little tra-la-la chord.

"Doom and destruction, Miss B?"

"Yes! And, forgive me for saying so, but they won't take kindly to the fact you like a glass, Mrs G. And all the rows and . . ."

"What have you been up to, you silly old thing? Have you been making trouble for us?"

"I have not! Sure and I'm telling you this for love of Maisie, and the job, and the rest of you."

She looked at me long and hard.

"When, Ruth?" she said.

"Tuesday, teatime."

She left the piano and walked up and down. Then sat down and played a thunderous bit, banging the notes out like the beast she is. I stood there awkwardly.

"Ha!" she said, over her shoulder, stopping with a jolt. "Plenty of time then."

I didn't know what she was on about. But suddenly I'd a hunch there was a chance for me to get a bit of what I wanted. I blurted it out. I told her there was something else. I told her I'd like to sleep in the house, just three nights a week.

"Good Heavens!" she said. "Why?"

"I'll keep to myself."

"Well, well!" she said, looking amused. "So this is blackmail? Let me get this straight. You'll help me to keep my Maisie if I let you sleep here for three nights a week? Good Lord! What about sins of collusion, conspiracy and corruption? You'll be saying Hail Marys for the rest of your life!"

"It's for the family's sake, Mrs Gowrie."

"You must be raving mad, Ruth Blane!"

I remained silent. I'd had my say. She was thinking it over, I could tell. She made a show of smoothing her hair, so I wouldn't notice that her hands were trembling.

"Tuesday afternoon you said, Miss B? Teatime?" Her voice was high again, like it was the night the lawyer came.

"That's when they're coming . . ."

"Don't worry about a thing," she said imperiously, with a dismissive nod towards the door. "Three nights? You can have your three nights, I suppose. *Andale*! Buzz off now. It's Saturday."

★ ★ ★

On Tuesday they came: Mrs Scott from the school and a Mr Miller from Social Services. When I arrived at half past four with Maisie you'd not have believed it was the same kitchen. The floor was scrubbed within an inch of its life and the table set with a fine tablecloth I'd never laid eyes on. There were egg sandwiches, freshly-baked scones and a big lemon cake – light as a feather. A silver teapot let off the smell of posh tea and she'd a jug of farm milk waiting beside the children's mugs.

But the mother herself was the biggest surprise. Lila Gowrie was wearing a tweed skirt which came down well below her knees and a baggy, knitted jersey. The riot of hair she always has floating round her shoulders was tied back in a knot. She had Edward Gowrie sitting there too like a tidy doll, in a jacket and tie with his hair cut and combed.

You'd think they'd have smelled a rat, but Mr Miller was looking pleased as punch with her fussing round him, passing the homemade jam, all gentle and motherly.

"We do so understand your position . . ." she was saying as we came in. "You can't be too careful in a case like . . . ah, Maisie dear, come and join our visitors! Miss Blane, pull up a chair."

Maisie looked round the room in amazement. Mrs Scott noted her amazement. I saw Lila Gowrie noting her noting it, and realizing she'd better concentrate her efforts on the woman. She leaned towards the teacher in a confiding way.

"It's a surprise for Maisie, you see," she murmured confidentially. "We don't often have strangers in. The family unit has become so important since, since . . ."

"Of course!" Mrs Scott agreed.

At this moment Flora came in. She opened her mouth wide.

"Wow!" she said, looking round, letting her school bag drop to the floor. Her mother, sensing disaster, jumped up to greet her.

"Mr Miller and Mrs Scott have come specially to see how Maisie is getting on, isn't that good of them?" she said, before Flora could go any further.

"Oh, yeah! I meant: Wow, lemon cake!"

"You mean you meant *wow* lemon cake, again!" Edward Gowrie offered up supportively.

"Of course I meant lemon cake again!" Flo said. "It must be Tuesday. If it was Thursday," she said conversationally to Mrs Scott, "We'd be having organic gingerbread and if it was . . ."

And on they went like a well-rehearsed team. I couldn't believe my ears. After a bit Lila gave Mrs Scott a woman-to-woman look and took her off to see round the house. For the life of me I'll never know what she said to her, nor how she'd cleaned up the whole place, but when they came back the teacher was beaming and Mr Miller was down on the floor playing Monopoly with Maisie and Edward while Flora and I were washing up.

★　★　★

When they left the family went mad. Flora rushed to the CD player and put on an Ella Fitzgerald song. Lila seized Maisie and danced round the sofa with her, then kissed her husband full on the lips. Flo grabbed me and tried to get me to dance: "Chill out, Miss B!" she sang out. "Let it happen!" When I pulled away, she collapsed in a heap with her father and Maisie on the sofa, the girls tickling each other and laughing their heads off. The last thing I saw was Lila Gowrie taking a bottle of wine from her store behind the encyclopaedias.

"I'm in heaven, I'm in heaven . . ."

It was a display, right enough. Foolishness! I slipped away. For one thing I don't trust that music.

★   ★   ★

I'd heard it before, a long time ago in a bar; well a café really, in Cork. Aunt Minna was at home with Mother. 'Off you go, Ruthie,' she said, giving me twenty punts. Twenty! 'Have a bit of fun for yourself.' I hardly knew what to do. I took the bus to Cork and headed for the shops. I remember that day feeling . . . ? What was it? Young! That's it, I felt young all over my skin. I bought a dress! It cost eighteen of the twenty punts. It was common material, bright red, with huge shoulder pads, the sort of thing Mother would never have in the house. I felt fine! I felt all of sixteen. It was then I heard music coming out of a building onto the street. I went into a café – or was it a bar? I'd never been in a public place by myself. I don't know what made me so bold.

There was a young man in jeans serving, an immigrant of some sort with dark brown eyes and an earring. I ordered a Coke but, when I got up to go, he said, 'Have one on the house, sweetheart.' He spoke in a foreign accent. I sat at a table sipping my second drink. I felt his eyes on me. I felt as if warm water squeezed from a sponge was dripping over me down the red dress.

I knew it was dangerous, like the fishermen Mother was forever warning me against. Ella Fitzgerald was singing that very song. *"I'm in heaven, I'm in heaven, and I'm so in love that I can hardly speak . . ."* I finished my drink, got up and left.

I never went back. Mother and her boyfriend Mr Padstow had done a good job of putting me off sex in their different ways. But, sometimes I think, what if I'd stayed? I was happy that day, full of myself and the tight touch of the dress.

The thing is when you've just the one parent, and you're filled to the brim with what's respectable and what's not, you're confused. The summer I was ten mother's friend, Mr Padstow, offered to give me swimming lessons. I was excited, filled with dreams of being like other girls and joining the sports club. "Trust me!" he said. "Lie on my hand and kick your legs." His was a mobile hand alright, more like an eel than a hand.

"Say thank you to kind Mr Padstow," Mother had said.

"I don't want to swim after all."

"You're an ungrateful little Toad."

"I won't swim!" I cried.

Not long after that, respectable Mr Padstow went back to his respectable wife.

★　★　★

It's a nice enough song, but her voice . . . it's not right at all. It's unsettling for a child. Wasn't I just a child myself, unsettled by Miss Fitzgerald all those years ago?

Ah, well, I'll be moving into Cleary Court for three nights a week! The authorities need never know . . . things will be changing round here. The birth mother will lose her hold. Maisie Gowrie will have me to keep her safe.

FLORA

I couldn't wait till I was sixteen. I had to go. Look at us – look at Ma! Take an evening like last night – back to what it used to be? I don't think so! It was heaven at the time. Ella Fitzgerald reminds me of the heaven it used to be. But later, much later, it was me that picked her up. It's a hard job lifting her, but I didn't want Dad to have to – and I didn't want Miss Blane prying into our business.

It's not washing Ma I mind so much, not really. It's seeing her so . . . sad.

It's Owen's fault – all of it. He's utterly, utterly selfish. Last night I made up my mind not to wait. Breen was sacked after the Haiti farce, the police are useless, Dad's giving up so there's no one else . . . I *have* to find him.

Call me a criminal if you like but, if you're going to find a missing person, you need money, right? It's obvious! How can you buy a train ticket without money? How can you find a place to live? How can you follow up on clues? I mean *hello* . . .

I took two hundred and fifty euros and fifty pounds in ten pound notes from Dad's drawer and two bits of jewellery from Ma's walnut box. Not stuff she wears, heavy things she must have inherited. One is a locket with such a big stone in the middle the tiny gold claws are bent crooked trying to hold it down. It's crying out to be sold. It's cool stealing for a reason, like taking the knife off a dead guard in order to stick it into a living one that's blocking your path.

The following evening I was ready to go. I squashed the money and jewels into my backpack with my music and three sets of clothes: everyday jeans and tops; smart stuff, as in grown-up smart – things you might wear to get a point across with a stranger and trendy gear, just in case I need it. I remembered my passport at the last minute.

★   ★   ★

The next part hurt. I looked in on Maisie. It was 4.30 a.m. Her hair was spread out on the pillow like the haze you get behind saints' heads in paintings. I found her board and wrote: 'Gone to get Owen! Flo.' I forced myself not to wonder what she'd think in the morning. It's about discipline, see. It's a quest. I have to be organized – and brave . . .

I tiptoed downstairs in my socks and opened the door. The moon was hardly there, just a faint thread of light. I should have looked up the weather forecast. I stood in the doorway shivering, thinking about Maisie waking up. I tiptoed back upstairs and put a lipstick kiss on her mirror.

Then I was out in the five o'clock dark walking to the garage where Mick works. I knew my way by the smell of the lane. I could tell where the wood begins by the trunks closing around me. Soon I was through the wood crossing the tufty field, the rocks looked weird in their night shapes. After that it was less scary, there was a furl of moleskin light over the sea and a flock of birds tossing about above the water like a handful of soot. Then I hit the road, and the petrol station was only yards away.

After a few pebbles my friend Mick woke up and agreed to take me to the station. I thought he'd demand a kiss but he only said: 'You owe me one, Flora,' and got back in his truck, slamming the door.

Half an hour later I was on the train to Dublin. We were off – and they'd still be asleep at home . . . I couldn't believe it! The train picked up speed, jumping the smallest roads like a fresh horse, pushing aside little blue fields till they clambered over their own stone walls and folded back into the misty light. I took six deep breaths and looked around.

Sitting across from me was the most elegant lady I'd ever seen. She was absorbed in her book, curled round it like a lynx. She was wearing a suede jacket, soft as the skins of the tiny, timid animals it must have come from. Under the jacket was a silk blouse open at the neck, no necklace, no fuss. I could see her tanned collar bone in the V of the flowing collar of the blouse. On her wrist, the one that showed, was a heavy silver owl bracelet. I peeped under the table to have a look at her feet. Boots, of the finest leather, moulded her ankles like gloves.

I was dying to talk to her. But she was deep in her book and didn't look at me.

"Gorgeous boots!" I said brightly after a while. She gave me a curious glance, and went back to her reading.

I tried again five minutes later: "You'll be accustomed to trains, then?" I said in my friendliest voice . . . "and travelling? London, Paris, Bruges – spots like that? And New York City, no doubt? You'll be familiar with them all!"

She looked up, surprised. "Well, some of them," she acknowledged, keeping her place with one finger.

"For no reason at all . . . a lady like yourself," I went on, "just for the pleasure of it, I expect; or to see the paintings? Or to be painted yourself? In those very boots, perhaps, with a chestnut filly by your side."

She laughed and put down her book. Soon she was listening and I was talking. Bit by bit I found myself telling her about Owen and old bigot Breen and how Dad was dragged off to Gaza.

Words poured out of my mouth to the lovely stranger with the sad face, things I'd never said out loud before, coming out of me in a rush, like rain, like a deluge of rain after days on end when the earth's baked dry.

But when I got to the bit about the photograph, the one of Dad on the front page of the *Examiner* supporting Mrs O'Neill at the airport, I stopped. She's in a stagger, almost falling over her own feet. And Dad looks small beside her – shrunk, like a jersey you've washed in the machine by mistake. His head is down and his hat's gone.

I bit my lip and looked out of the window.

Just then the man with the food trolley came round. That helped.

I was famished. I bought four Kit-Kats and a Coke.

"I'm Claire Rossmore" the lady said at that point. And you, my dear, are . . . ?" She was looking at me a little strangely. I remembered the need for secrecy.

"Flora Maud O'Casey." I tossed it out without hesitation for love of *Juno and the Paycock* and Mr Sean O'Casey himself. The Maud was for Maud Gonne, of course.

"So you are looking for your brother?"

"I'm representing the family," I told her proudly.

"Does your mother know you are representing your family?" She asked?

I explained that my mother wasn't well. I told her I was going to the source, where Owen had been studying only one and a half years ago. I explained I had a clue which, naturally, I couldn't divulge.

"Naturally." She agreed.

But then she was back on the same subject, more insistent than before, asking me again if my parents knew I was on this train.

"Look!" I told her, "You can't be expected to understand my mission if you haven't got a missing person in your own family."

"Oh, but I do," she said. "In a way I too have a missing person. My life is not quite the cosmopolitan, cultured haven you envision, Flora, I am, as it happens, missing a son – and a granddaughter, Although they may not seem like missing people to you . . ."

There was a pause. A wash of red started at the level of her neck, rising upwards, suffusing her face, causing her large grey eyes to glisten.

". . . but when the person you love most in the world hates you, they disappear from your life. There's no accident, no mystery, no death, but they won't see you or talk to you. You don't know your own granddaughter – you've never once held her," she added faintly.

"That doesn't count!" I shouted.

I told her it wasn't a real disappearing act like my brother had brought off, messing up lives, making a father lose his tongue and a mother take to drinking wine like it was tea. I told her Maisie didn't have a mother anymore because her own one was out of it, missing stairs, falling-down, throwing-up . . . I told her Miss Blane said that if we didn't watch out they'd put Maisie in a home, not home as in *home*, the other kind, the kind that smells of carbolic soap with baby letters on the wall.

I stared at her, swallowing hard, trying to keep my face steady. I ruffled through my bag and took my eye shadow out and began painting my eyes with purple stardust, but little rivers escaped and made their way down my cheeks. I was gulping, crying like a baby.

Now, I don't know why I was so mean to her. Now that I've learned about men that don't come back from wars and people who forget their own names after accidents and children, snatched from the sweet green grass they are playing on and sold for sex into the heart of cement cities . . . I realize that I shouldn't have been so harsh.

There are masses of them, you see, masses of families waiting and hoping and hoping and waiting, doors left unlocked at night, windows left ajar and candles lit. The pain of it seeps through the world like spilled oil clogging the feathers of sea birds till they sink and are washed up on the beach like wrung-out rags.

Mrs Rossmore handed me a handkerchief and a card with her Dublin address on it.

"You may be right," she said quietly, "but you should know it counts for me."

★　★　★

I spent the whole afternoon trying to find a lodging house. Mrs Mollohan was my fifth try, ageist like the others, but she went for my story. I was getting better at lying. My fictional parents abroad had become so real I almost loved them. I told her I was a student at Moran's tutorial college. The name Moran's clinched it. It just came to me. She didn't want to admit she hadn't heard of such a likely-sounding place.

★　★　★

The room had nothing in it but a single bed, one chair, a mirror and a steel stand with six wire hangers. Our rooms at home are full of things: elephantine armoires, old desks, paintings, piles of books, paper and pencils. There's a basket of turf in every room and a fire for when it's cold. Lorca, my old grey cat, sleeps on my bed. He lies across me at night like a soft, ticking cushion.

There was just one window in the room. It wouldn't open. It looked onto a brick wall. My window at home is so big that the outside comes in. I wake up when there's frost on the ground and the room fills up with bright, white dazzle. Even when there's rain, and the trees outside are dripping, a greenish light casts a forest of watery shadows over my walls.

I stood in the middle of the room thinking of Ma. I felt a lurch in my stomach. I wanted to be sitting at her dressing table while she combed the tugs out of my hair. *Hija, tranquilita!* she used to say. That's Spanish for 'daughter, calm down!' It's her mother tongue. I could go downstairs and phone her – I could be home tomorrow, I thought. Then I remembered she hasn't used these words lately, not in a long time actually, not since Owen left. I thought of the fights and remembered why I'd come. It was getting dark and I was hungrier than I've ever been in my life. I went out and found a café. I ordered an all-day-breakfast with eggs, sausages, chips, tomatoes and fried bread and a big mug of cocoa. It made me feel great again, ready for anything. The waiter was a know-it-all boy with slicked-up hair and black trousers two sizes too big for him. I told him I was tracking down an important person.

"Yeah?" he said, "Forget it!"

"Why?"

"You're a kid. You should be in school, that's why."

I ignored him, another ageist, not a day over 17 himself. The next day I set off with my 3 clues.

Owen's landlady's address.

Desmond Hamilton's address – a friend who was in Owen's band.

The Green something?? Pub where they used to drink – so one word was missing, but I remembered Owen telling me there was a photograph of Seamus Heaney and Michael Longley on the wall.

It was a disaster. I showed a photo I had of Owen coming out of the sea at Ballyloe to students with musical instruments under their arms – no one recognized him, the landlady said she wasn't in the business of remembering all the boys in her properties and she certainly couldn't recognise a half naked boy with seaweed in his hear. I did find Desmond, but he was just back from 2 years in Peru and didn't even know Owen had vanished. Nothing led to anything else, like it does in books.

The fifth day I was slumped over a hot chocolate back in the café with the same waiter.

"So how's the hot-stuff-spy-school-dropout today?" he asked, with a smirk. I ignored him, then . . .

"Do you know a 'Green *something* Pub?'" I asked on impulse, since you should question anyone, even the Taliban, who might supply information.

"You mean The Green Arms?"

He did. And it was right. The very pub Owen had described to me. The boy added it was a hang-out for poets and musicians. He added the drinking age was 18.

"So what?" I said in my coolest voice.

"They won't let you in, that's what."

"Oh, yeah?"

"Oh, yeah!" he went back at me.

I was out of there in minutes: laughing, running, skipping, spirits soaring . . .

★　★　★

The next morning I started planning how to get into the pub. OK, being fifteen was a drawback, but if Ma could turn herself into a dowdy county lady what was holding me back from putting on a few years? I tried on my trendy outfit, the pretty rose skirt I'd made from one of Ma's scarves, my black top and net stockings. I looked alright, but even with purple stardust my face was wrong. I put my jeans back on and slipped out. After asking around I found a shopping centre where a woman was doing make-overs. I asked her politely if she could make me older.

"Whatever would you be wanting that for?" she said. "In my born days I never met a girl after more years, there's plenty after less."

"It's for a play," I told her. "I'm to be eighteen, with a look of experience."

She did it then, grumbling away. "They're after me for a ready flush and full lips when their own are like a length of washing line," she complained. "Now you come along asking me to undo what the good Lord gave you!"

All the same she lengthened my face, lost my cheeks and even changed the shape of my eyes. I looked great! I ate three sausage rolls on the way back to celebrate, trying not to smudge my mature lips. I lay on my bed waiting for it to get dark.

★   ★   ★

A mass of people were queuing up outside the pub. I hung about nervously trying to attach myself to any group that would have me. A girl called Cilla noticed me. She had a neat green stripe in her hair and a tough confident face. "Hey, kid! Want to come in with us?" she offered. The guys she was with looked like they'd had a few already. One, called Finn, was as hairy and orange as an orang-utan and there was a Billy in falling-apart jeans, who didn't say much, just lit up and gave me the once-over. They were OK with it. When our turn came we were swept into the smoke and noise together – no sweat.

Soon I was drinking, something that looked like juice but wasn't and sailing along somewhere I'd never been before. There was a sea of conversation going on round me, the trouble in the

Middle East, how Auden was influenced by the States, Nigerian women writers – something about a Belfast judge who'd committed perjury. It was *so* real. Awesome! The place had graffiti on the walls: cartoons of Paisley and Gerry Adams and a photograph of Heaney talking to Ted Hughes at this very bar. Nobody seemed to mind me being there.

Then I saw an odd thing. At one of the tables, a pale girl about my age was sitting with a much older man. The man was wearing a suit, he was leaning forward talking urgently. The girl was looking doubtful, her body language was like 'not sure.' There was a bottle of water between them, and a plate of digestive biscuits.

A boy, well a man really, was standing beside me. He was bending down curiously, watching me watching them.

"Strange, don't you think?" He said quietly.

"Creepy!" I said.

Have you seen but a bright lily grow
Before rude hands have touched it?
Have you mark'd but the fall of snow
Before the soil hath smutch'd it?

He quoted the words in my ear in a low voice. It was spot on. The young girl didn't look like me. She looked as pure as the snow in the poem – and doubtful.

"Did you write that?" I asked him.

"No, someone called Ben Jonson did 400 years ago, but it's what you're thinking, perhaps?"

"But the guy, the man she's with? He's so old!"

"Yes," he agreed, sadly, "so old."

He drifted off, leaving me feeling very young. Somehow another of those drinks was in my hand. I started it without meaning to. My mouth was full of the syrupy taste. My head felt like candy floss. I saw a used glass and spat the second mouthful into it when no one was looking.

Cilla was with me again, asking me if I was from Dublin and what I was up to. I told her about what had happened and how I was looking for any trace of Owen. She listened, asking questions, getting into the whole thing, but Finn, the orang-utan, kept interrupting, coming on to me, pushing into our space.

"Get off, will you? I'm not a pick-up," I said.

"Well, you don't look like the Virgin Mary to me." His arm was round my waist, his leg was rubbing mine.

"Did I say I was the Virgin Mary? I pushed him away as hard as I could.

"What's with you, Finn?" Cilla asked. "Can't you see she's only a baby dressed up in her sister's clothes?"

I saw red. I'd liked Cilla – really liked her. I'd thought she was cool. I told her I was *not* a baby and they were *not* my sister's clothes. I told her the top was the latest thing from Midleton and the skirt was sheer silk and she should be so lucky. I told her my mother was a dresser, the toast of the town.

The poet, who was called Patrick, appeared again – the one who'd quoted the verse about soil and snow.

"Hey, calm down! Cilla's only trying to help. What *are* you doing here anyway? Who are you, little creature?"

I tried to think clearly, he might be ageist too for all I knew. I was afraid my mature mouth must have been washed away by the sweet drink. I could feel my cheeks coming back.

"What *is* your name, he asked?"

"Marina Mar O'Casey Gonne."

"Mmm," he said. "Unusual! An infinitely romantic, if totally unlikely name. It matches you perfectly!"

"Look," I said. "Don't *you* laugh at me."

"Oh, I wouldn't dare," he replied gravely.

Then he asked me about myself and if I was studying in Dublin.

I told him bits about me and Owen, looking up now and then at the most beautiful fellow I'd ever seen: brown wavy hair, and a mouth that waved too, following my voice, changing from thoughtful to amused, then back to thoughtful.

But when I got to the word *missing*, the grey in his eyes darkened and locked onto mine in sympathy – or was it anger? It could have been anger. He was so tall I came up to the concave bit where the chest starts on a boy – or a man? He was wearing a shrugged-on jacket over a ragged jersey and boots.

I hoped he'd stay close, listening to me forever, but the drink had made me dizzy and I was beginning to lose track of my own story. Besides, things were happening in the pub, the noise was growing. Then, all at once, chaos broke out.

The man, the older man in a suit, was on his feet shepherding the pale girl out of the pub when Finn and another fellow blocked his path.

"Y'fuckin' fake!" Finn shouted at him.

"You cunt-catchin', bible-bashin', mind-fuckin' . . ." shouted the other boy, pushing him so hard he fell.

The man's glasses flew through the air and his briefcase was knocked clean out of his hand. A bouncer was there in a flash pulling the boys off. 'Sorry, Sir!' The publican apologised, righting the man and helping him to his feet. The girl made for the door by herself, trembling and uncertain.

"Wow!" I said, "What's this about?"

"It's a conversion you're looking at, Marina," Cilla said. "It's young malleable minds they're after. She'll be in South America or one of those places before you know it."

"It's a package deal," Patrick said bitterly. "No make-up, no hash, no sex and in return you get travel and a first class ticket to heaven."

It was over. The man was on his feet again, pink and flustered, looking round for the girl.

The door swung open and, for a minute or two, I saw her standing outside on the pavement, lit by a street lamp. I could see her face clearly. It was a searching, needing face, full of longing. It reminded me of something I'd seen before, but I couldn't remember what.

The man was being escorted out. When the girl heard him coming, she drew her hair back and fastened it with a clasp. She seemed to be bracing herself, as if she was trying to be brave.

It was then that I remembered what I'd forgotten. She reminded me of my brother two summers ago, his last summer with us. Owen's skin had been deathly pale like hers and his eyes had had the same anxious look.

The man claimed the girl. He took her by the elbow and walked her away. Rain blurred their figures but I noticed she was holding back, in fact he was pulling her along, you could call it dragging. I ran to the door to get a better look – but they were gone.

Patrick was beside me again.

"What's an epiphany exactly?" I asked him. "Like with Stephen Daedalus, when he saw the girl in the sea with her skirts tucked into her drawers?"

"A moment of illumination?"

"Yes, yes . . . I think I might have had one. Will you help me to find my brother, Patrick?"

"How can I help a girl with a name woven from dreams? You'll vanish if I let you go. Where would I find you?"

"The Shelbourne Hotel at ten am. tomorrow!" I said, in a moment of inspiration. It was the only place I could think of. I'd been there years ago with Dad and Owen.

We were close together, looking at each other.

"Oh!" Patrick said softly in my ear.

"Oh . . ?"

He bent his head and, for an instant, his lips were on my lips. It was more of a stroke than a kiss, the sweep of a paint brush, dry yet not absolutely dry at the same time.

Then I was off – racing through the rain, dodging my way back to Stoneybatter and Mrs Mollohan's upper room. 'Wow!' I thought. 'It's all happening! I'll tell Ma! I'll tell her I'm onto Owen. I'll tell her I've found a footprint in the sand that might fit Owen's. I'll tell her I'll have her boy back soon. I'll tell Dad, too . . . I'll tell them all. I'll sing a song down the line to Maisie. I'll wait till it's sure – after breakfast with Patrick tomorrow, when I'm hot on the track. Won't Ma be proud . . .'

I was lost in the rain for a few minutes, my hair was soaking wet, my skirt stuck to my legs like wet butterfly wings . . . then the cafe with the ageist waiter appeared and I recognised my street. "I'll tell them there's a boy, a man – a gentleman if they like – who is helping me. Dad will be over the moon."

As for Patrick! His jacket smelled of poems and his eyes were storm warnings when there's a gale force wind on the way. I'd felt the yearn of a saxaphone between us. The sweet, aching sounds that draw you in. I danced the last block, splashing in puddles. Before I put my key in Mrs Mullohan's door I turned my face up to the night sky and let the rain run into my mouth and pour down my throat.

MAISIE

Owen! I woke up sweltering. A mass of spots like hot red ants were creeping over me. I tried to cry "help," so Flo would hear. But spots were stuck down my throat, so the words didn't come. Spots were winding round my tummy and chest, they were creeping up my neck and hiding in my hair. I tried again,

"'Help!"

I couldn't see for bright day was coming in the window and my eyes hurt. The light was as sharp as glass. I got out of bed and felt my way to Flo's room, but she wasn't there. Then I ran, almost falling, to Ma's room. She was sleeping a deep sleep. I stood close to her head.

"Help!" I said again, almost crying. Nothing happened.

"Wake up, Ma! It's me, Maisie."

She didn't open her eyes. Her skin was as white and her eyelids pale as ice. Her eyes moved a little under the skin.

"Not now, Maisie, Go away . . ."

Then I was running and tripping and slipping and falling all over the house looking for someone to take care of me. I couldn't see where I was going. Tears stung my spots.

★ ★ ★

A big, fat, hand was holding a damp towel on my forehead: 'There there, Maisie. You're back in your own bed now. Isn't that grand?' The curtains were closed. The room was shadowy and cool. "It's all right darlin', we'll chase those spots away, you'll see. They'll be running for their life in no time." Her voice went on in drifts like light snow. One of my arms was lifted up and patted with calamine lotion, dab, dab, the dabbing went under my arm where a nest of hot spots were itching

— dab, dab, dab. My arm was back by my side on a tight clean sheet. "It's the measles you've got, hush now, those horrid spots won't stand a chance!"

Bit by bit of me was dabbed and dried and put back on the sheet, the sheet was smooth and cool. The big hand lifted my head so I could sip some apple juice. I opened my eyes a little, the curtains were closed, but slowly my room unfolded and I could see my board; 'Gone to get Owen! Flo' was written on it.

'Now, go to sleep, there's my good girl. I'll be in and out and round about.'

I wanted to tell her, but I couldn't reach my board. Miss Blane was leaving. Her huge body in its flowery dress was tip-toeing out of the room.

"Miss Blane!"

She stopped.

"Miss Blane," I said a little louder..

"Did I hear my name?"

"Flo's gone to fetch Owen. He'll be home soon!"

She came back and read the words. Then she was by my bed again, looking down at me.

"You talked to me, Maisie Grace Gowry," she said. "Well, well, well, isn't that a wonder! What was it took you so long?"

Her smiles floated round the darkened room like sunbeams. They fell onto my bed and landed on my pillow.

★　★　★

MISS BLANE

I found Maisie stumbling round the house with a high fever, confused and crying her heart out. I lifted her up and carried her back to her room. She had a bad case of the measles. I tended her like a mother. Later, when I was leaving her room, believing she'd fallen asleep, suddenly I heard my name: "Miss Blane!" I stopped, wondering if I'd heard aright. "Flo's gone to fetch Owen," the child said. "He'll be home soon!" There was a peal in her little voice, like Sunday morning church bells sounding out across the fields. Her voice was pure and sweet. It was the first time she'd talked to me. Her sister was gone; I was the one she told!

When Lila Gowrie got over her hangover, she read the message on Maisie's board, examined her broken-into jewel box and let out a wail like you never heard in your life. The colour drained from Edward Gowrie's face as he, too, read Flora's message. He looked unwell that day, his breathing was bad, but he got dressed immediately and went to the police station.

★   ★   ★

The house is in an uproar. Its two days now that Flora's been gone, *two* days. We've to concentrate on getting her back. And now Madam tells me I'm needed: "She can count on me in this crisis to look after her Maisie," she tells me. "I'm to be sure to follow the Dr's instructions: a light nourishing broth from one of the organic chickens – not the ordinary ones." She goes over every point a hundred times. She can count on me; of course she can, if I don't kill her first.

In the evenings she drinks and weeps and drinks – and weeps.

I'm to stay within reach of the phone. It hasn't rung yet. The house feels like a husk with the fruit gone. What is it about that Flora? The child has a way of filling every room when she's here. If she's washing her hair in the nursery bathroom don't we all know about it? When it's rinsed she shakes it out like a wild mare and lets the drops fly. Then, leaving her music playing full blast and an unholy mess on the bathroom floor, she runs downstairs with nothing on but a towel. She'll be after some favour, no doubt. There's nothing empty about this house with her around.

★ ★ ★

It's the third day – three days now since Flora left this house. Even I am worried for her, out in the world on her own. She's a scrap of a thing, but developed. That's the danger with young girls these days, they've a body on them doesn't match their brains. It's trouble, with the creeps there are about today: grown men on computers, immigrants, new-age travellers, out-of-work policemen and fishermen. Don't imagine you can trust a fisherman – off a boat from who knows where.

She's only a child really, with a sweetness about her, 'though I say it myself, as like to fling her arms round your neck as she is to create a scene. She's too trusting by far. She'll flirt with a stranger for the fun of it. Her skirts are far too short. Her legs are far too long.

Maisie is up for the first time. She's been busy all day carrying Flora's old cat out of her sister's room into her own, making a nest for the hairy creature in her pretty cushions, fetching its water-bowl, fetching its blanket, bringing sardines up from the larder – back and forth, back and forth.

I was about to get her back to bed when the sound of hysterical sobs reached us from downstairs. Above the noise Edward Gowrie's strained voice could be heard trying to calm his wife. Maisie put the cat down and stood silent and still. I thought things had changed between us, but when I tried to console her she was unapproachable. She pets the cat and sings to it – but I'm back where I was, not another word to me.

When I went downstairs later the Gowries were sitting at the kitchen table looking like victims of an earthquake. Flora running off like that had stopped them dead in their tracks. They hadn't eaten a proper meal since she left, so I took pity on them and made a chicken casserole from one of Lila Gowrie's cookbooks. It cost me, I don't mind saying, those fancy recipes of hers are a lot of fuss and bother, herbs no ordinary mortal's heard of – but they have to eat, don't they? They'll be needing their strength.

During the meal it was Edward Gowrie doing the talking for once. 'It's alright, Lila, dearest. It will be alright,' he promised. "Flora will have a plan, we can trust her to have a plan." He reached across the table and patted her hand. "Come on dear, try a little . . . Mmm! Tarragon . . . Lila, I believe this sauce has tarragon in it!" He cut up a bit of chicken and put the fork in her hand.

★　★　★

Today is the fourth day since that selfish little minx took off. This very afternoon Mr and Mrs Gowrie are off to the television studio in Cork with photographs of their daughter. It's an occasion, you'd think? Well, normally speaking it would be. National exposure on Irish television. It could lead to satellite – they could be seen in The United States of America!

A car is waiting for them at the end of the path. It's not the little one she takes to Tesco. I never knew they had a proper car; turns out they keep it in the old stable under a cover. It's an old Jaguar – British Racing Green! Edward Gowrie was up at seven this morning charging the battery, cleaning and polishing, making a *sssss* sound through his teeth as he worked. I was back and forth with soap and water helping the best I could.

It's the first time I've seen them out together, but it's not what you'd think. Lila's not dressed for the event. She's no make-up on and I can tell it was him combed her hair for she doesn't normally have a parting. The new parting cuts through her savage hair like a modern road through flat land. She looks more like a hospital patient than a lady, walking with little steps, taking her husband's arm.

I still have them in sight. They've just reached the Jaguar. Mr Gowrie has his arm tight round his wife's waist. Her head's flopping against his chest. Now he's bending down. He's lifting her into the car.

★ ★ ★

FLORA

Breakfast at the Shelbourne was not like I expected. I mean no romance, positively *none*. I don't know what I had expected, there hadn't been time to expect, but I'd imagined there'd be *something*.

A stranger met me in the lobby. He looked totally different, not like a boy or a student or a poet, not the rumpled, touching-me person who had drawn his lips across mine the night before. He was wearing a tweed jacket of all things, and the sort of trousers a friend's father might wear. You'd have thought he *was* a friend's father, if he wasn't so gorgeous.

I'm not saying he wasn't friendly, but it was like he was just doing a job and I was the client. Before we'd even got our poached eggs (two each, sitting on crumpets covered with mind-blowingly delicious hollandaise sauce) he was asking questions about Owen. He took out a pen and wrote notes, making me repeat bits here and there. Only when we'd finished did he stretch out his long legs and give me a smile, a nice enough smile, but so *not* like last night's.

"Before we go, how about a few facts about you?" he said. "Just tiresome little details like your real name? And where you are staying? And might I trouble you for a telephone number?"

I gave him the information, reluctantly. Then he asked if I had friends in Dublin.

"Sure!" I said.

"Sure?" he repeated, looking at me doubtfully.

There's something strange about the way he looks at me – it's curious and anxious at the same time, unlike the sexy poet in the pub or the parent figure in a tweed jacket.

"Sure," I said again.

There was silence between us. I didn't like lying to him. I have to lie, obviously. It's about getting where you want to get. It's fun, normally, but it felt bad with Patrick. Not that he believed me, I don't think he believed me for a minute.

"I have an idea, Flora." he said after a while. "It's a long shot, but I'd like you to meet a man I know. He's the father of a disappeared girl who was studying here – a year before your brother."

At that moment I didn't care about the man with a missing daughter and, to be honest, I'd almost forgotten about Owen. I could only think: *Hey! I'll see him again.* I felt as if a hard sweet had burst open against the roof of my mouth and the taste was swamping through me.

"Thanks," I said, trying to act cool. He offered to pick me up the following day at 4 p.m. on the corner of my street.

I dawdled on my way back to Mrs M's. There were hours to fill in until 4 o'clock the next day. I couldn't bear the thought of my room with the view of wall. I hated the coat stand and the smelly fitted carpet. It was raining softly. I sat down on a bench under a ceiling of leaves and thought about home.

Tomorrow would be my eighth day away. Something told me that four days for me wasn't the same as four days for them. Parents with a missing son and an absent daughter would find it . . . longer. I tried to comfort myself by thinking of my 'Gone to get Owen! Flo.' message. But the more I thought about it, the less comforting it seemed. They would be wondering *where* I'd gone and *how* I'd got there. As for my lipstick kiss it showed affection, yes, but it wasn't exactly hard core evidence of anything at all.

There were two voices in my head. The first said: "It's cool, Flo! Don't worry about a thing – ring them tomorrow." The second voice, which might have been God's, said: "Flora Gowrie, ring them *now*! You know perfectly well they will be anxious and, by the way, what about the money? And what about the jewels?"

But I simply couldn't ring until I had something hot to tell them. Tomorrow would be easier. I thought of their faces and began to feel very scared indeed. A wind got up and zigzagged down the street bringing a sweep of solid rain. The branches above my head shifted ominously, a clump of sodden leaves fell on my head.

★ ★ ★

Patrick's a genius! He filled me in on the way to the meeting. He'd found out that Owen was at University at the same time as Cristina Warren-Barnes, the girl who went missing before he did. Apparently they actually *knew* each other. He told me about an organization in the USA called TTG which stands for TURN TO GOD. It's a cult. Mr Warren-Barnes thinks he might have found a link between his missing daughter and this place.

It was all happening! Me and Patrick in an office listening to a father who is trying to track down a daughter. I mean *Wow*! Mr Warren-Barnes is a domineering sort of guy, small and solid like a dressed-up wrestler. His big cheeks join up with his short neck and double chins and the whole thing is squashed into the hard collar of a posh business shirt. He doesn't look fat, just hard to move like a sack of flour. He told us his wife had a massive breakdown when Cristina disappeared and has to be cared for. I noticed a silver-framed photo of a girl on his desk. She didn't look the type to vanish. She looked pretty and hopeful, a cashmere sweater and pearls sort of girl.

Mr W-B has been searching for his daughter for months. An exit counsellor, a man called Alan Corvin, suggested they should investigate TTG. Now Mr W-B is into studying it himself. He told us it has the most sophisticated mind control tactics of any comparable organization, only now, he said, does he feel ready to take them on.

"Take them on?" Patrick asked.

He started to explain . . .

"You mean like a swat team leader?" I interrupted. "Surprise assault, to get the person out?"

"In some respects," he said cautiously.

It opened up then – my questions and his answers. He was friendly at first, but when I got to Owen and all the searching we'd done, he began to back off. I wanted him to realize Ma and Dad are going through the *very same thing* . . . and he wanted me to know that Cristina is a special case and about all the research he's done, the months of work . . .

"But *we* need help."

"I'm afraid I'm not in a position to help you," he said, firmly.

The air thickened with hurt. I felt my chest tighten. Owen seemed to be fading again; the path between us was overgrown, I could barely see it. Mr W-B turned to Cristina's photograph for reassurance. I followed his gaze. She was less distinct now, a mist blurred the hopeful lines of her face.

Patrick's voice brought us back to earth.

"Thank you for your time, sir," he said. "Miss Gowrie and I are most grateful. We would appreciate a chance to meet your exit counsellor ourselves. My father sends his regards and hopes you will be able to arrange this."

His father? I didn't get it, still don't. It's a total mystery. Why *is* Patrick helping me, anyway? What's in it for him?

Whatever, it worked! His father's regards made an impression. "I'll see what I can do, Patrick," he said as he showed us out. "But don't get your hopes up – it's a complicated business."

The minute the door closed behind us Patrick took off his

jacket and tie and shook himself like an itchy horse.

"Shit!" he said. "Not bad for a first time!" But a minute later, he announced he had to rush off. I must have looked desolate. He seemed annoyed for a minute; perhaps he was thinking 'Is this part of the deal? Do I have to look after her too?' But then he shrugged and said:

"You can come, if you want. It's about something I wrote. It's at Cilla's – some friends . . ."

Of course I wanted! I tried to look as if I might have something else to do, but before I could think of anything he grabbed my arm and pulled me along after a moving bus.

"Come on – RUN!"

When we arrived at Cilla's there were about 10 people there already – sexy men in their twenties and a few clever looking girls. Patrick caused a bit of a sensation. He'd just had some poems published – everyone was telling him how great they were, urging him to read. He had a beer and, after a bit, opened his book. His voice was deep and strange. It made me think of turned earth and the sinking blade of a plough.

If losing is more
Than finding,
If the found
Is lost?
If the found
Is apart,
If the apart
Is parched?
If no water flows
There,
Where
She is.

There was heaps more. But I didn't get it. Who is the *she?* Who is found, or lost? When he'd finished his friends gathered round saying *penetrating* and *devastating* and the evening turned into a party, not a normal party with music, it was more about people shouting out opinions and drinking straight vodkas from little glasses. Patrick was flushed with pleasure, swigging it back, handing out copies of his thin book of poems.

After a while most of them drifted off. We were lying on an old beanbag half-watching the news on television. Patrick had just stretched across me for a beer, as he straightened up his eyes drifted into mine and paused; he seemed to look at me properly for the first time since the pub . . .

That's when it happened.

Suddenly I *heard* Dad's voice! "Our beloved daughter . . . fifteen years old." I jerked up and looked past Patrick at the TV. I caught a quick glimpse of Ma standing rigidly beside Dad. I should have thrown a fit to distract Patrick; I should have shut it off, or launched myself across him. But it was too late – too, too late. A photograph of me filled the screen, vast and babyish.

How could Ma have done it? The photo she chose is from ages ago. It's one she loves of me in Owen's garden. No one normal would recognize me. But Patrick knew it was me straight away. He leapt up, aghast.

"Flora!" he said. "*Fifteen!* You're *fifteen* years old! I had no idea . . . haven't you spoken to your parents? Don't they know where you are?"

"No, I mean I was going to, I planned to, right after the meeting – I wanted to have something to tell them, but . . ."

"That's not good enough, Flora!" He was furious, red in the face, glaring at me. "How could you be so selfish? *Think* of what they are going through . . ."

It was scary. Patrick *so* mad at me, when only a minute before we'd been on the edge of being close. Now my parents had ruined everything.

Yet Ma and Dad's faces had taken me aback too. They looked like cartoons of themselves, stilted and peculiar. It was the last thing I thought they'd do . . . even Owen didn't get the TV treatment. And Dad had said *beloved daughter*, as if I was dead, as if I was a name on a tombstone.

"Ring them!" Patrick roared. And he was out of Cilla's flat in a flash, slamming the door behind him.

MAISIE

Owen! You've got Flo on her way to get you. Isn't that grand? I have it on my board. There's no one knows her way like Flo. On Mayday we were coming back from Fred's beach. It was late with the sun going down. It was another path, not the usual one, and the rocks were other rocks. "Isn't this the wrong path, Flo?" I called out, for she was up ahead. 'Not wrong, just different,' she shouted. 'It'll take us back.' The night sky was crouched and waiting like a black cat. I could hardly see my feet. "Flo! I can hardly see my feet!" I shouted. "Don't worry," she sang out, "I'm at the gate already." And it WAS the same gate, the mossy one that needs a lift. She took my hand in hers and we ran home.

In Scripture class, Peter asked Jesus: "But how will we know the way?" And He was after telling him, "I am the way, the truth and the light."

Flo's smarter than Peter. She's never lost, not even in Cork.

It'll be grand when you get here, Owen. We'll have yellow cake for tea. The house will be back, like it used to be. You'll be in your room and Flo will be in her room and I'll be in mine.

I had the measles, Owen, then Flo left. Now there are doors opening and shutting like words in my head. Ma and Dad went out in the green car today. Imagine that! They'll be back soon for sure, for all the lorries and clatter. They'll find their way.

Flo will bring you home, Owen! The day you arrive I'll be upstairs. If I'm not upstairs I'll be in the garden. If I'm not in the garden I'll be in the kitchen . . . it will be like it used to be, won't it? Ma will have tea ready – she'll have lemon cake and a fire on the go.

Flo's on her way to fetch you back. I have it on my board.

CHAPTER
5

MISS BLANE

I'd just got Maisie to bed when the telephone rang. It was Flora all in a fluster, talking her head off, not a thought for the terrible trouble she's caused.

"Oh, it's you! Hello, Miss B. Where's Ma? Call her now, will you? and get Dad, too. Hurry, please! I need to speak to them right away. I've great news . . ."

"Flora! Where are you? For the love of God, tell me where you are?"

"If I told you that you'd be after me like a pack of hounds," she said with a laugh.

"It's no laughing matter, you selfish, thieving, mindless girl. It's worse than hounds you'll have after you before long."

"Look! Just get them, OK?"

"Your father and mother went to the television studios this very day, Flora, with pictures of your cheeky face that's causing all the trouble. They're not back yet. There's been a policeman up here and no end of fuss and bother – your precious Ma's hardly taken more than a cup of tea since you left."

"The police? But I left a message on Maisie's board. Ma and Dad knew why I went. They know I'm OK."

"Knew? Know what? They don't know a thing. You're a girl

of fifteen, not a paid detective. Where are you, Flora? Tell me right away!"

There was silence at the end of the line.

"Is Maisie safe?"

"Safe! Of course she is. She's upstairs in her bed where you ought to be."

"Ma? Did she really? I never thought . . ."

"Of course she minds, Flora. You're only a child. You're a missing person now, just like your fool of a brother. You don't know what you've got, do you? Your mother loves you, even if she is a lunatic. And you've a father made of solid gold."

There was silence. I was afraid the line had gone dead. But her voice came back again, fainter than before.

"Tell them I rang, Miss Blane. Tell them I'll pay the money back, and the jewels . . . tell Ma I haven't sold them."

"Flora! Now you listen to me . . ."

"Tell Dad I'm getting help, from a ma . . . from a responsible older person."

"Where *are* you, you stupid, stupid . . ."

"Comfort my mother, will you, Miss B?" There was the sound of swallowing and the line went dead.

★ ★ ★

They weren't back till half ten. I was up and waiting. Lila Gowrie was all for walking right past me but her husband stopped. "Good evening, Ruth," he said, politely.

"She rang!" I told them. "Flora rang!"

That stopped her dead in her tracks. She turned to look at me. I swear I never saw such unearthly hope in a face. I repeated the conversation word for word. I told them what she'd said and what I'd said.

"But where is she?"

"She refused to say."

"You should have made her."

"I tried, but she wouldn't say. It's all for you, don't you see? It's not about the boy. It's to get you back . . ."

"Back? Back from where?"

I was tired. They were exhausted. I shouldn't have let go at her like I did.

"You might ask yourself that, Mrs Gowrie. She's not had much loving from you, has she now? She thinks it's because of your beloved Owen. It's as clear as day to me, she thinks if she gets him back it'll be like it was before – the bacon she's always on about, the fire going, family games, an end to the drinking."

For a moment the woman stared at me. When she did speak it was in a measured, restrained voice, and the more deadly for it.

"Thank you for your analysis, Ruth Blane, but there's a lot you don't know. You have no idea what it is to be a mother. You don't know a thing about missing people . . . you don't know about loving them. I doubt you know about loving anyone. Above all, you know nothing about my feelings for my daughter."

"I know what I know," I said, trying to hide my hurt. "I've eyes in my head, haven't I?" I caught the smell of alcohol on her breath, they'd have stopped somewhere on the way back.

"You can't show me my mistakes with all your pseudo-psychology," she went on, "for I know them myself. But I'm beginning to see yours. They stick out a mile. You are a parasite, a bitter, frightening woman feeding on us in our sorrow. Eddie!" she said suddenly. "Carry Maisie to our bed, *now!* And put a lock on the door till I get there."

Her husband looked anxiously from her to me, then back at her. He lowered his head submissively and went upstairs.

"I don't want you near my daughter, Miss Blane. I want you gone in the morning."

★ ★ ★

Later, I was slumped over the kitchen table, not crying for goodness sake, but I felt as if she'd taken a stick to me and I couldn't fight back. I was angry, angrier than I've ever been. I'd been there for some time when I heard the shuffle of bedroom slippers.

"Let me make you a cup of tea, Ruth."

It will have been the tea set me off and the man's kindness for, of a sudden, I was breaking apart right there at the table.

"I never had what she had," I burst out. "The Lord never gave me any part of it. I never had a husband nor children like her. Never felt my waters break, never knew the glory of a birth pang – not a one. Ah, how I'd have loved the fierce ones, an infant of my own making moving down my body."

"I know, I know . . . it isn't fair, Ruth," his agitation showed in his hands, which shook as he put a cup of tea in front of me. "But you mustn't believe her. She's a sick woman. Alcohol destroys what once was. In the morning she'll have forgotten she sacked you."

When I didn't move he pushed the cup forward a little, but pity for myself overwhelmed me.

"I have breasts like her, don't I? I have compassion . . ."

"Of course you do," he muttered, embarrassed.

"*She* doubts I know much about loving – *she* doubts. Can't she see what's staring her in the face? Can't she not see that I love the daughters she tosses aside like spud peelings?"

"It wasn't always like this."

He glanced at my untouched tea, got up, searched for the

sugar bowl and set it before me with a spoon. "There!" he said. "There we are, now drink your tea." I wiped my eyes and sipped the tea.

Across the table I saw an old man in love with his wife.

"What was it changed her then?"

"She's not entirely changed . . ."

I spared him nothing. After abuse like that what was the difference? I asked him where she got her claws from. I asked him what a good man like himself was doing married to a bitch who didn't even watch out for her young.

"It wasn't always like this," he said.

Gradually it came out of him – a story that stopped and started and moved from soft words as he remembered the good times to silence as he reflected on his present trouble. He'd been invited as a young man to fish at an old house in Donegal. That's where they'd met. He described Lila at twenty-six, well he tried to but he couldn't find the words. He just opened his hands and looked at me and shook his head, the marvel of her beauty filling his eyes. She had never been to Ireland before, he told me. She loved the house in Donegal, the bay, the seals and the fishermen in the evenings.

Would you credit that? I thought to myself. *Fishermen . . . the stink of the fishermen . . .* words engrained in my mind. But it seems the young Lila Gowrie, for all her beauty and piano playing, loved the fishermen.

"Indeed?" I said.

He told me he had been a shy young man, without much experience of life. He said he watched her for two days with hardly a word between them and then, to his surprise, he'd felt her watching him from under the folds of her eyes.

I'll bet she was, I thought to myself. The young Edward Gowrie, eyes blue as a summer sky, with a house to inherit, a profession at his fingertips and not a blemish on his fair young face. I could see it all: the gentlemen with fishing rods and expensive green boots up to their thighs, poached salmon and lemon butter sauce in the evenings, their hands circled round brandy glasses . . . I don't watch the BBC for nothing. And her just another immigrant, taking up a good English girl's place in a proper orchestra. *From under the folds of her eyes, my hat!*

I made another pot of tea. It was two in the morning. I was half dead with exhaustion but I could hardly leave, could I? There was no stopping him now. He described a marriage like something out of a Hollywood film. She lit up his house, he said, her voice, her music, her dramatic stories, her cooking and then, most precious of all, they were blessed with three beautiful children.

It must have been at that point that reality struck, for there was a long pause. Poor soul! It was as if the present was barking at his heels and he couldn't hold it back. He tried to go on, but it was some time before he could.

"You see Ruth, of the children it was our boy she held most dear. From a very young age she spoke to him in Spanish. He learned her language in a way the girls never did. They'd go out in the boat together – and cribbage . . . I think it was cribbage they played in the evenings."

He wandered on, reliving the past. When the lad was thirteen, he started slipping from them both, particularly his mother – his friend's death was the cause. That would be the Doherty boy, I thought, shot through the stomach when his uncle's farm was raided in Donegal. That family was up to no good, mind you. It was an older brother they were after, but young Billy they got.

"I should have understood that where there's been loss . . . "

"Loss?"

"Yes, my wife lost her brother, you see. It was a political thing.

They never found out what happened. It was in Spain, a long time ago. The family had to leave. I should have remembered. I should have noticed her fear."

"Ah, don't go blaming yourself. That'd be when she started the drinking, then?"

He didn't answer. He didn't speak for a long time.

"I failed to stop my son from leaving, you see. Now my sweet Flo has gone to find him."

He looked around the kitchen, his Adam's apple moving up and down, panic in his eyes.

"I can not find two of my three children," he said at last. "Nor any trace of my wife."

FLORA

That night, the night I rang home, Ma and Dad were still out. I got Miss B. It was useless, an *impossible* conversation: her putting me down, lecturing me on-on-on, wanting to know where I was, and me hardly holding it together. I could imagine her standing in the hall beside the oak table with the heavy vase that always has branches in it. There would be fallen leaves on the flagstones, there always are. Maisie would be asleep upstairs. I could see it all. She told me that Ma minded so much about me going that she wouldn't eat . . . I felt worse and worse. I've failed to get anywhere, I've made Ma suffer. I've enraged Patrick. I was sure he'd never speak to me again.

I was wrong about that. Patrick does speak to me. He speaks to me quite a lot, in a technical sense that is. He speaks as a friend, in a kind-older-person helps irresponsible-younger-person way. There's zero contact. His eyes don't look *into* my eyes. They look *at* me, as if I was a chair or a mug of tea. A mug of tea might be better . . . Another thing, he never touches me, even by mistake. I feel like a leper. I mean he goes to great lengths *not* to touch me. I've never yearned, but there's a yearn in me now, a longing for the feel of him. Yesterday the first few buttons of his jeans shirt were open and I found myself wanting to put my hand inside the collar, flat against his warm skin. How mad is that? It's debilitating. It's sick!

I should be totally happy and concentrated because so much has happened and most of it's good. I've been moved for a start, no more wall. Patrick came to Mrs M's one day and just said, 'You're out of here!' Now I'm staying with his father in the house where he was brought up. I love it – there's a fantastic library, proper meals and a dear Irish terrier called Bluff. Patrick's father is Dr of Divinity at the university. He's an academic with masses of work. I get given assignments instead of having to pay rent; things like: 'Go to Trinity College and take a picture of the bust of Jonathan Swift.' At first I didn't see the point, but now I realize it's an education thing. He worries about me not being at school. He cares about me learning stuff, so I try not to disappoint him. He's formal, but sweet when you get to know him. We talk about everything under the sun on the nights we have dinner together.

Amazingly Dr Herbert has actually spoken to Dad. He assured him I was in good hands. I'm not sure how he did it, but he seems to have got it across that the Owen project is moving forward and I'm an essential part of it. I've talked to the parents too. I've apologised for clearing out like I did. I'm beginning to realize Patrick's father is a bit of a saint. It's because of him Mr Warren-Barnes speaks to us at all – and because of him we've finally met the exit counsellor, Alan Corvin.

Alan was so not what I'd imagined! He has slightly sweaty hair which stands up like a punk and wears dead cool clothes: black jeans, a black T- shirt under an ancient suede jacket and Nikes. He looks more like someone in a boy band than a 35 year-old trained psychologist who specializes in negotiating with priests, kidnappers, prison guards, politicians and so on. He arrives at Mr W-B's office on his Kawasaki bike, strips his kit off, tosses it on the prissy sofa and gets going. When he talks its spot-on stuff. Nobody argues.

I've been getting to know Alan by myself too as he's dead keen to find out about Owen. We meet in the meadows and he fires questions at me as we jog round. It's difficult answering things at a run, but that's what he's like. He asks about Billy's death and Owen's relationship with Ma and which poet he loved most and when he started smoking hash – that sort of in-depth thing. He wanted to know if I'd ever seen him with anyone unusual. I wasn't going to tell him about the pub people and the woman, but he has this way of making you trust him completely – so I did.

Then, two days ago, we had a mega breakthrough! I still can't believe it. Alan called a meeting in Mr Warren-Barnes office. He said he'd got us all together because he'd accumulated enough evidence to suppose that Cristina *and* Owen were involved with TTG. We hardly had time to take this in before he mentioned he was in favour of me going to Arizona – *if* it could be arranged, *if* I got permission. *Me? Go there . . . ? Surreal!*

Mr W-B exploded: "But I know nothing about this young lady! What age is she anyway? Where are her parents? I couldn't possibly be expected to take . . ."

"She wouldn't be your responsibility, sir!" Alan cut in. "She'd be mine, under an assumed name of course, a candidate for TTG so far as anyone else knew. She'd be in the initiation centre, not the main building."

"You mean as a spy?" I asked, breathlessly.

Alan smiled at me. "You could say that, kiddo. This is pretty unusual stuff. But we're not there yet, no way. We need your parents' permission – that's a big one. Then there's a bigger . . ."

"What about her safety, Alan?" Patrick interrupted. "What if they brainwash her?"

"Trust me, Patrick. I wouldn't make this suggestion if I thought she'd be in danger. I'll be there – in the motel with Humphrey and Felicity Warren-Barnes. I'd be able to get her out long before they got their claws into her. The thing is we've got a good little actress here. She'd have been great in the cold war, this girl of yours! And we hope she'll be able to help with Cristina's case too," he said, turning to Mr W-B.

Everyone started talking at once, clamouring for his attention.

"You guys have to hold your horses," Alan said. "Parents often refuse permission and, even if they go for it, what about the money? Who'll pay for Flora?"

I hadn't thought about that. It had never crossed my mind there was a chance of me going anywhere.

"I propose to pay, with my father's help," Patrick said quietly.

I stared at him in amazement. Mr W-B asked what on earth it had to do with him?

"Empathy," Patrick was saying. "Call it that if you like. My mother disappeared from my life when I was a baby, but that's not the point. With respect, Sir, you have been through so much pain yourself you must understand how desperate the Gowrie family are to get their son back? It's critical we stop these people."

"Well, what do you say?" Alan said, looking round with a challenging smile. "Shall we have a go? Shall we try to get these kids back?"

★ ★ ★

Half an hour later we were sitting in a pizza place in an emotional daze. Although the pizza was delicious, Patrick's words were hitting me over and over. *How* could it be true?

"You'll . . . pay? You said you'd pay for me?"

"Yes."

"But why, Patrick? You're a poet. You aren't rich – you've got your own life?"

He got that ruffled look men get, that mannish thing when their ears go red.

"Your brother – getting him back; it happens to be something I mind about. I'm lucky enough to have a trust fund."

I was still flummoxed. I asked him if it was true about his mother.

"It is true, only worse. I mean my situation is different. My mother buggered off, leaving us – the difference between your missing person and mine is I *want* mine gone."

"But – but how can you say that?" I was looking at a different Patrick, angrier and more vulnerable than before.

"Look, d'you really want to hear about it?"

I nodded, a little nervously. It was the way he'd said; 'I want her gone,' that got me. He finished off his Guinness, ordered another and started telling his story. At first it was matter-of-fact like a history lesson. Patrick can cope with facts, including difficult ones, like me. But even he changes when facts fail, when ice is so thin you don't know if it will hold your weight and you can't tell how deep the water is below.

Apparently his mother wasn't the sort of person who would leave a tiny baby and a husband she loved; well she'd *appeared* to love them, his father still believed she had. But she went, all the same, leaving nothing behind except a note with instructions about her baby's next bottle.

"Bottle?"

"Yes, Flora, baby's drink out of bottles if their mothers don't want to feed them. If they are off fucking passing American journalists the baby gets given a bottle!"

I'd never seen him like this.

He'd got the story out of his father bit by bit. When he was little his father described a perfect mother: *She told stories that made people laugh. Her face was like a flower. Animals loved her.* Patrick would ask him why she wasn't at home making them laugh. He wanted to see the flower face. He wanted to show her the dolphins he'd seen in County Clare. But his father wouldn't say more, so Patrick learned to stop asking. When he was a teenager he brought it up again, begging his father tell him what went wrong. His father maintained nothing went wrong. 'But what about me?' he would say. 'Didn't she love *me*?' Finally, his father admitted she'd left with an American friend. 'Why didn't you get her back?' Patrick had shouted. 'I tried,' Dr Herbert had said. 'I failed.'

"You must have wanted to find her yourself?"

"I did. That's just what happened. When I was sixteen I took off – like you."

We sat in silence. I was imagining a little creature with rumpled hair forever searching for a face like a flower.

"I suppose you want to know what happened?" Patrick asked me, almost aggressively. "I don't talk about it. Why should I tell you?"

"I care," I mumbled.

"You'd better hear this, then. My father realized I had to go. I think he'd always known this would happen one day. She was living in Brooklyn, New York, at that point."

"Did you warn her you were coming?"

"Did I hell! I stormed in ready to confront her and blame her and kill whoever she was with. But it wasn't like that. I found a delicate girl-mother all alone in a big studio surrounded by sculptures. She was wearing dungarees, dusty with chalk and wood chips. When I told her who I was she stood very still and stared at me. 'Did I make you?' she whispered, touching my face with fingers which smelled of varnish. 'Did I really?'

We spent hours together but got nowhere. I was cruel. I asked her how easy it had been leaving a husband who loved her and a small baby. "I couldn't stay," she said. "Why not?" I demanded. "Was it because of another man? Was that why you left?" 'That wasn't it!' she cried out. "I didn't connect. I don't . . . connect." She was sitting cross-legged on the floor, more like a child than a mother. I didn't understand a word she was saying. I found out she'd lived with many people in many places: Brooklyn, Soho,

103

Vermont, Canada – but mostly in what she called *nowhereland*.

I was very young and very hurt. When I was about to leave, she said: 'Patrick! Have you understood what I'm trying to say? Nothing lasts. I don't know how to make things last.' 'But I was your baby!' I cried. "You're a freak, not a wife or a mother!" "Babies throttle you." were her last words to me. "They cling – they are the worst . . ."

"So you see, I didn't get her back."

"It must hurt . . . dreadfully."

"I'm glad she's gone! Get it, Flora? It's over. I don't fucking care."

MAISIE

Owen! We had a poem in school called 'The Road Not Taken' and the teacher explained it was not about roads at all, but about choosing one way to go and forever wondering what the other one would have been like. Well, I've been thinking about what road it was you took and hoping there'll be a turn in it soon to bring you back.

I heard another poem in school today. It was about me. It was in the playground after school. Suddenly there were three girls tight round me like a belt. They were Elsie Allen's lot. I tried to walk away but Moina was in front of me and Isabel Campbell was to the right and Elsie was blocking the gate.

"We've a pretty poem for you, Maisie Gowrie," Elsie said, "seeing how you love the poetry class." Then they sang it out.

> *Her brother's gone*
> *Hoot, hoot, hoot*
> *Left his sister*
> *Mute, mute, mute . . .*
> *The second bit was about Ma.*
> *If you want to find her Ma*
> *Take a trip to Murphy's . . .*

I couldn't hear the rest because Miss Blane charged into the circle whirling her bag round her, scaring the life out of the girls. She'd come to fetch me home and had seen us there. The kids were sent to Mrs Scott.

"Are you alright, Maisie?" Miss Blane asked me. "That'll teach them a lesson they'll not forget!" She looked great, big and pink and panting . . . her red hair stood up like a bunch of wild spaghetti. "Did

you know that after a battle the victor can have anything she wants for tea?"

I did not. She took my hand and we were off. We had scones and raspberry jam and two slices of almond cake each and a cone from the ice-cream van.

That night Ma sat on my bed. She said the girls weren't poets because poets were beautiful, intelligent people and Elsie Allen looked like an English pudding and couldn't write for toffee. She said the poem they made up was meant to be funny but we could invent a funnier one with our eyes shut. So we shut our eyes and started off . . .

Elsie Allen doesn't know it
But she sure 'aint a poet!
Moina and Izy are under her thumb
The 3 of them are dumb, dumb DUMB!

We would, politely
Like to mention
They got detention
While Maisie G
Went out for tea
Ha Ha! He He hee!

We giggled. Then we snuggled up and I fell asleep.

CHAPTER

6

MISS BLANE

It was just as Edward Gowrie said. The very morning after my dismissal I was needed: asked to make a trip to the farmer's market, told to pick up tickets for a concert, expected to take Maisie to her piano lesson – a fine way to treat a body after a sacking. I'd like to see them manage without me. No apology, mind. Oh, no! *Sorry* is a word her ladyship failed to pick up in the English language for all her witty quotations. I could demand one, I've a right to an apology – but I let it go. I'm well settled here. Mrs G has no idea if I'm sleeping in her house for three nights a week, or seven. If she can take liberties with our arrangement, well then so can I . . .

The Gowries have heard from a Doctor of Divinity who teaches at the boy's old college, letting them know Flora is a guest in his house and they are taking good care of her. She's been on the phone too, with lots of sobs and sorrys. Now it seems there's possible news of the son's whereabouts – it's an emotional rollercoaster round here with all the goings on.

Last week I was told they were expecting a visitor for lunch. I thought from all the fuss it was to be Dr Herbert himself so, imagine my surprise when a fellow who hadn't shaved in a week stormed up to the house on a motorbike: black leather trousers, studs, zips, silver helmet . . . goodness knows who he is or what he's after? You'd think they'd want to know why their daughter's mixing with his kind. I wouldn't trust him as far as the kitchen sink, but Mr and Mrs G were closeted in the library with him for hours. Next thing I knew he got an invitation to spend the night and, before he left on the Monday, he was allowed to take Maisie to school on the back of his bike, as though he was a member of this family . . . I *was* shocked.

Since that young man was here there's been a change in this house – something you'd never believe – a joke if ever I heard one. Lila Gowrie is trying to get off the alcohol. She'll *never* make it, of course, not in a month of Sundays. Still it got me to thinking . . .

I'm not sure it would suit now, not sure at all. If she was straight and sober she'd be giving lunches and supporting orphans and getting photographed at the races. She'd be wanting the curtains interlined and running me off my feet. If she was on the wagon she'd be on at me for certain: she'd notice things, she'd have me sleeping at the flat . . . she'd be claiming Maisie back.

When Edward Gowrie is out on his teaching nights and Maisie is asleep I see our new abstemious AA member like a cat on hot bricks. Once she's stopped roaming about and changing things from one place to another she sits in the library pretending to read. She's a good enough actress, but she can't conceal the shakes. She can't hold her book steady. It's not hard to guess what's going on in her head – and it's not what's in the story.

Last night I decided the time had come to intervene. I dropped by to see to the fire.

"A nightcap, Mrs Gowrie?"

She didn't answer. I could tell she'd heard me, but she didn't look up from her book.

"Can I get you a drink, Mrs G?"

Her long slender fingers grasped the book fiercely. There was no visible change in her demeanour, but I felt her will-power waver like a reed in the wind. I poured a generous glass of wine into a wine glass. I poured it slowly, knowing she was listening, knowing the sound of liquor falling is like the angelus to her. I laid the glass on the drum table beside her with an almost full bottle of Sauvignon Blanc beside it and quietly left the room.

Not an hour later she, and the bottle, had gone! Well, what can you do? They'll find a way . . .

It's a great lark having the place to myself! Last night, I steamed pictures of Maisie as a baby out of their photograph book. I smelt the book. I smelt their youth. I saw the missing boy's face, beautiful in its way, blond hair like his father's must have been – but he's not a real lad, too delicate by far, narrow shoulders, thin wrists and long unmanly fingers. I put the book away and lay on her sofa resting my feet on her cushions. I drank a cup of posh tea from one of her fancy cups. It was a good evening right enough, nothing more or less than I deserved.

★   ★   ★

Little did I know then that I'd a surprise in store, a surprise which could alter my life. A letter came from my mother's sister; well not from her directly, it was written by the matron of an old people's home up in Galway. My Aunt Minna would like to see me; could I manage the journey there? I was pleased as punch. She was the one who stood up for me when I was little and gave me the only cuddles that came my way. I lost sight of her when her husband Bobby died and their farm was sold.

I told Mrs G I was off for a few days. 'Take as long as you like, old thing,' she said. 'We'll trundle along very well without you!' She'd no need to be so rude – just let her see how much there is to be done. That Donnie of hers is past it, daft in the head, nigh on ninety if he's a day. He can't get down on his knees to scrub and if he does get down he can't get up. He'll be smoking his pipe and toasting himself by the fire, giving her an earful of his complaints while she spoils the life out of him.

I caught the bus and by evening I'd found Hydrangea Hills, a charitable institute for the aged and infirm. I almost walked past my aunt in the hall. The tanned, cheery face I remembered had collapsed into folds of skin, soft as soapsuds, and where there'd been a mass of auburn curls, a few strands of silver hair were brushed over her freckled scalp. But for all that she was as kind as ever, kissing and petting me as if I was her very own daughter. A carer made up a bed for me in her room. I'd brought some sherry and biscuits and we had a grand evening together.

In the morning, when they took round the tea, I got to asking about my father.

"Respectable?" She giggled like a girl. "More like in with the morning catch and out with the mended nets."

"What . . . ? The only father I ever heard about was somebody Blane, a businessman?"

"Ruthie darlin', I thought you'd want to know. That's one of the reasons I needed to see you again before I join little Bo and Bobby up there where all the promises are kept. Your father was a fisherman and none the worse for it."

"But . . . but my mother would have nothing to do with fishermen. *The stink of the fishermen.* It was all I heard, day after day."

"Wasn't that just like her?" Aunt Minna said. "Your mother left home when she was fourteen, farming or fishing they were all one to her – *inferior.* She was after the posh life, not about to be dragged down by us O'Leary's. She must have hated herself for falling for your Dad, a big Nordic chap with hairy arms, off one of the boats. It was only after he'd sailed away, leaving a small bump behind that turned out to be you, that an unearthly miracle took place. It would match any thing you've read about in your book of saints – a transformation!"

"A transformation?"

"Nothing less! The man I'd seen on your mother's stairs with my own two eyes, the one who left his cap on her dummy and two fresh herrings in her fridge, turned overnight into a Mr Blane who no one had ever seen at all; a respectable upholsterer, married to your mother in a small private ceremony. I have the letter still!"

"You couldn't fault her for want of imagination," I said sourly.

"No indeed, she could invent a pope if it suited her. She'd every detail worked out. She was forever telling us that Norman Blane was a *gentleman,* tragically killed in a car crash before your birth on an urgent call to attend to his sofa business."

My aunt was laughing – and soon I was laughing too. I'd never cared much for the sound of Mr Blane. Wasn't one absent father as bad as another?

"Bobby and I wanted you to bide with us," she said, "but she wouldn't hear of it."

"I was needed."

"Yes! And an almighty shame that was. She was a tyrant, if I ever saw one. Thank the Lord you're nothing like her."

I kept quiet. "If she only knew," I thought. "I'm a traitor to my profession. The lust for a child is overwhelming me."

Before I left she handed me a post office savings book. Almost fourteen thousand euros! Aunt Minna had been saving for me since her baby died. Forty-five punts one Christmas, twenty the following March, on and on, year after year, punts becoming euros, little sums mounting up. I stared at the book in amazement. I'd been to their farm as a child. She didn't even have a fridge. They had an outside lavatory with a bucket of lime.

I hugged an armful of frail little aunt – and wept.

★ ★ ★

On the return journey I couldn't tell if I was dreaming or awake. As the bus hurtled back to Cork images flowed through my mind, as bright and clear as a full moon over the Irish Sea. I am there! I see myself clearly on the night ferry from Rosslare to Fishguard. My body is moving to the sink and sway of a big boat as it churns forward, knocking waves aside like old bricks, creating blossoms of surf on either side. A child's sleeping head rests against my breast. The sleep is induced, just this once, it's my own girlie, I know what's best for her.

At Ennis it got colder. It would have been the door opening and shutting for the passengers that wanted out. I stayed in my seat. Someone had left a newspaper across the way. The word *Kidnapper* caught my attention. It's a harsh word, to be sure, and there's some that use it mistakenly. I looked at it again: *Middle-aged Kidnapper Steals* . . . You've to ignore them, I thought, There's a conspiracy of police and paparazzi out there, waiting to get you. They probably don't know the real story. They wouldn't recognize an act of compassion if it was staring them in the face. There might be a kafuffle at the time, but it all comes right in the end.

I got my coat down from the rack. It's heedless folk cause the draft, you see, making the sensible passengers shiver. Finally we were off on the last lap. I shut my eyes.

Look! There I am in my little house in an English town. I see myself, clear as day. I'm working. Up with the lark, getting my girl's lunch box ready. I'm cutting neat strips of carrot and celery like the posh mums do. There's a ripe apple going in and a bottle of milk and a chocolate bar for a treat. My child's off to school with her hair well brushed and her clothes neat and clean. I wave goodbye and smile at a neighbour across the way. She smiles back. I'm a single mother and proud of it. Single mothers have stature these days – they're all the rage!

★　★　★

That night I looked in on Maisie, I smoothed her hair and tucked the sheet round her. I bent down feeling the child's moist, even breaths against my cheek. I leant closer and kissed her lightly, lightly on the lips – a mother's tender caress.

I hardly slept all night. Aunt Minna's money was kindling in my mind – it set my dreams alight, it set the old craving off again. From a very young age, slaving for *her*, maybe fourteen years old, maybe younger, the craving for a baby was deep inside me – an empty space inside me calling out, with a cry all its own.

Back then all I knew was sewing, so I sewed in secret. Little things for a baby: yokes, puff sleeves, tiny jackets, and booties with an appliqué stripe . . . I hid them in a drawer where her wheelchair couldn't go. But one day Mother noticed a small pillow slip, too tiny for her customers. She recognized my stitches and guessed what was in my heart.

"Don't tell me!" she said laughing, "my Brat wants a little Brat!"

When she had calmed down there followed questions as she established I wasn't pregnant.

"You silly, silly, silly creature," she said. "You need a respectable husband to have a baby. You need money! You need looks, and style. You have no style, Brat de-ah, and you *never* will! You couldn't attract a proper man if you tried."

She was thoroughly entertained. I remember her laughter, and her scorn.

"Now, put that idiotic thing away and get on with Miss Camilla's bridesmaid's dress."

She was right about the man. I hadn't got a man, proper or otherwise, and I didn't want one.

★ ★ ★

But this time it's different. The craving has a shape. It's for a single, sweet, freckled face, eight years old with hair the colour of turned barley. The child's eyes are somewhere between green and blue, too serious you might think for a child, but I'm the one knows how to soften the green and how to light up the blue. She needs a proper mother and aren't I born for the job? Hasn't the money for it been put into my hands? It will be God Himself sent me to Cleary Court. It's got me sewing again. Only this time the pattern's size 8, with room for growth.

When I fold her clothes warmth travels through my fingers, smoothing out the pain in my knuckles, it travels up the length of my arm, till it eases the stiffness in my neck. When I watch her eat the supper I've cooked, the ache that's been inside me these long years dissolves like sugar in a pan of simmering water.

FLORA

Alan went to Cleary Court to get permission for me to go to the USA. "All set, Flora!" he said when he got back. But I could tell by his voice things weren't *all set* and pestered him until he told me more. Ma had been stunned when she realized there really was a chance of finding Owen. Her first reaction was wanting to go herself. Typical! Alan explained why it had to be me – he'd outlined the plan – me posing as a young person interested in joining the cult.

"She's quite something, your Ma!" Alan interjected at that point.

I took that to mean she'd been in one of her flirtatious moods. Thank God I wasn't there.

"Oh?"

"Tragic too," he added. "I tried to help her – I mean over the drinking."

"What?"

I was astonished. Nobody, but nobody, talks to my mother about drinking. She invented the words *in denial*. But somehow funny old Alan, with his way of getting to the point and showing that he cares, had got through to her. I gather he was invited to stay for the night. He must have spent most of it talking to my parents.

At breakfast the next day, when they got down to the real reason he'd come: *me* going to the USA, *me* being fifteen, *me* missing school – well, Ma was a pushover apparently, all set to sign the permission right away.

"Typical!" I moaned again. "My mother would sell me down the river any day if it meant getting Owen back."

"That's not it, Flora! She believes in you. She thinks you're stronger than all of them put together. She wanted to hear every detail: Mrs Mullohan, you getting into the pub, Dr Herbert, Humphrey Warren-Barnes – she laughed out loud when we got to him."

"Yeah? How about my father?"

Alan frowned and scratched his head. "Yes, well I don't feel so great about him, kiddo."

"No?"

"He may sign, but I think this whole thing's a bit much for him. He didn't like the sound of the place, hated it actually. And he's upset about someone else paying for you, although he couldn't – and wouldn't. He's right, of course – spot on. I'd like you to go home for a few days to talk it over with him, OK?"

"Did you mention Patrick?" I asked.

"There's nothing to mention . . . is there Flora?"

I never blush. What happened to me then wasn't the sudden colouring that happens to women in novels. It was more like being swallowed whole by a whale, being right inside its hot, pink mouth.

"Is there?" Alan repeated, looking at me suspiciously. "That would put a different slant on things."

"NO!" I said emphatically. "*I wish,*" I thought to myself, as the colour slowly subsided.

"D'you want out, Flora? It's not too late. "

"Of course not!"

So I went home and loved up Dad and hung out with Ma and Maisie. During those days I fixed the things I love in my mind: our rocks, the enormous pewter vase for branches on the hall table, our dear old toys and Lorca, he's nearly eighteen now, I love every grey hair of him. We went for a night picnic on Ebbie's cliff. It's the best family thing we do.

Dad has been slowly, reluctantly, won over to Alan's plan. He gave me an odd talk about being true to my own intelligence and protecting myself from influence. "Owen may not be able to be rescued," he said mysteriously. I didn't understand, until much later when I remembered his words. Things were speeding up. I hadn't expected it to get real so fast – there was only a week to go.

★　★　★

Mrs Warren-Barnes was detailed to buy me suitable clothes, suitable for a godly cult, that is. She's a timid little whispering, person who is in awe of her husband. She had a list of what they approve of at TTG and got me to try every single thing on, even hair bands. We bought knee-length loose shorts and blouses with Peter Pan collars, plain underwear and a boring shift for the evenings. Hair has to be tied back and no make up is allowed.

I'm sure it's *not* what Jesus would want. I remember the bit in the Bible when He is sitting *at meat* with the Pharisees and along comes a woman with a tremendously precious box of ointment. It must have been a bottle actually, because she breaks it open and pours it over His head. The Pharisees start dragging on about how expensive the ointment is, saying the money should be used for the poor. But Jesus tells them *she hath wrought a good work on me*. Clearly He's loved it! She's the attractive Mary, the one who is in love with him at the end. I bet Jesus doesn't want girls wearing knee-length shorts. I bet he doesn't want us putting ourselves down.

After the shopping she invited me out for tea. Mr W-B has her living in a home because of her nervous disposition. It's so mean. She's terrified of annoying him and asked me not to tell him about the left over tea cakes. She wrapped them up individually in paper napkins to take back to the other ladies. When it was time to go she made me promise to be very, very good. She wept a little and gave me a silver cross to give to Cristina. A van with a driver arrived to pick her up.

★ ★ ★

On my last day Patrick invited me for a picnic in the Wicklow Mountains. We drove the first part then left the car and began to clamber up a rough track. He talked about the history of the place and the rivers which have their source there: Liffey, Dargle, Slaney and Avoca. As he spoke, I imagined each river beginning as a burble in boggy ground, then finding its way through these hills, growing bigger all the time, and finally spilling joyfully down into a valley, drawn irresistibly towards the sea.

Later, in the harsh hotness of the desert, I tried to summon up Patrick's voice, the way he'd pronounced Dargle and words like Gaval-Rannall, Cualann and Cill Mhantain – but I couldn't get it back.

He walked with a long stride, lifting his curious face from time to time to look at birds, pointing at things with his hazel stick. I was concentrating on keeping up and not talking, letting the smells and sounds and the nearness of Patrick sink into my soul, when suddenly I spotted a peregrine.

"Look! A peregrine," I cried. He stopped and looked.

"Yes," he said, "a female."

"They're bigger than the males, aren't they?"

"They are, indeed."

He stopped and smiled at me, surprised and pleased. We stood still for a moment in a sweep of mizzle, bound together by the bird. Then we walked on.

★ ★ ★

Our picnic place was a grassy dent with bracken and hill behind and a stone wall sheltering us on one side. After we'd eaten our sandwiches and hard-boiled eggs and drunk a Thermos of leek soup we lay on our backs on an old tartan rug looking up at the sky; just lay there like two marble figures in a sarcophagus.

I longed to know what he was thinking, above all what he thought about me. Not knowing again – it kills you more slowly than knowing does. Roberta Flack's beautiful song *killing me softly with his song* says it all. I didn't have my iPod with me but it was playing in my head:

Strumming my pain with his fingers,
Singing my life with his words.

Patrick, this mysterious person lying beside me? In the pub that first time, attraction tugged us together, like the pull of rope in a tug-of-war game. I *know* he felt it too. But, since then he'd changed. I'd seen hurt and anger inside him and questions swarming about like confused bees.

He sang as if he knew me in all my dark despair
Then he looked right through me as if I wasn't there
But he was there, this stranger, singing clear and loud -

It was worse than any pain I'd known, him lying so near me, yet not near me at all? I had to find out what he was thinking. I simply had to risk *knowing* before I left. I sat up and looked in the opposite direction so that he wouldn't see the love in my eyes.

"I understand why," I said. "I mean why you're paying for me, Patrick. It's because of your mother, right? Obviously! I mean what else? I'm not your girlfriend . . . or anything. You don't want me to be anything."

He didn't speak at first. It was agony, like people on television shows waiting for the result of a DNA test.

"There you have it wrong, Flora!"

I kept on looking the other way. There were clouds merging, and not quite merging. A slant of late sunlight settled on the tumbled-down wall beside us where cows had clambered through a gap. *I'd got it wrong?* I imagined the cows nudging and pushing to get through.

"Turn round!" he said. I turned, keeping my eyes down, not daring to look . . .

"Flora, darling, look at me!" He got up and pulled me to my feet, staring right into my eyes.

"The word *darling* spread itself inside me like spilled honey.

"Can't you see? There are problems . . ."

"Like what?" I said. "You mean because I'm not beautiful or clever enough, or patient or . . . ?"

"No, none of these things! How could you think that?"

He held my face between his hands. "I'd love to be *anything*, as you put it, to you."

"But the problems . . . ?"

"We could call them circumstantial," he said. "Major inconveniences, like the fact you were an underage run-away when I met you, which puts me in the position of being an accessory. Think about it! I did not report you to the police. I've lied through my teeth on your sweet behalf. In a court of law little words like *abduction* might crop up and, if you were also in my bed, there's a bigger word that would have me locked up for a very long time."

He wrapped his arms around me. He put his lips against my neck.

". . . but, if I'd been seventeen?" I said after a while.

"Don't ask me that, Flora! You have a job to do. You are going to Arizona. You are going to try to bring back one disappeared person out of all the thousands, for your family, for all of us. Just give me one underage kiss and bloody well don't ask me again what would have happened if you'd been seventeen."

He held me so tightly I felt all of him against all of me. I felt a strange urge to lie back down on the tartan rug, but we remained standing, clutching each other. His mouth bruised my lips against my teeth. His tongue slid round the tip of mine and mine slid round his, like two slippery, silky, madly loving snakes.

We walked back to the car without talking. Patrick was back in his older person skin, but the kiss lay between us like a live thing, crimson as the last shreds of sun which were sinking into the Irish Sea. It had happened! It was there for me to remember and remember again in the girls' dormitory of Turn to God's initiation quarters.

MAISIE

It was grand when Flo was here, Owen. After she'd talked to Ma and Dad there was time for a favourite thing. It was a night picnic up on Ebbie's cliff. Flo and me were down on the shore collecting mussels, jumping from pool to pool, plucking them from the rocks. When we found a cluster we'd pull – they tried to hold on with little thread arms but we pulled harder and off they came and we dropped them into our pail. They were navy-blue and sea-blue streaked with white and curved like spoons. They were mostly tight shut – some had a bite of seaweed clenched in their shell mouths.

We climbed up the cliff path with the pail full and extra ones in my skirt and, when we reached the top, there they were – Ma and Dad sitting together on a rock with the sea swallowing the sun and a trembly moon staggering up into the sky. Dad had the bonfire hot and ready with a big pan on the grill. The mussels opened up the second they hit the bubbling butter. Ma squashed a lemon over them and shook in a scatter of parsley. We ate the inside part with scoops of sauce, lots and lots of it.

D'you remember, Owen? Do you remember the thud the waves make far below when they hit the rocks? And the way the spray flies up the cliff and over the edge wetting our faces? And d'you remember the sea-taste of mussels? And how it is being there in the dark, just our family, with stars coming out in a lovely rush?

We couldn't see each other properly, just butter-striped mouths and pink seafaces. Bits of moonlight hit the surf and caught on our cold bare feet.

Ma and Flo sang a song about a young girl who loved a handsome, winsome Johnnie more than painted rooms or silk stockings. Then Ma sang alone. It was about a letter from a man who was off in England looking for gold. He was homesick for Ireland and a lady called Mary. He should never have left, should he, Owen?

I don't remember walking home, just waking up the next day with the salty-smell still on my fingers. Now Flo's gone and Miss Blane is back. I'm making a garden for you, Owen. The flowers in the middle are white. The wall round them is navy-blue and streaky-blue. The shells stand up like spoons.

CHAPTER
7

MISS BLANE

It was chance she was alone – or circumstance. The word they used was neglect.

That Tuesday, Tuesday 3rd April, I dropped by the flat to pick up some sewing. A letter from Social Services advising me our reviews were starting on Wednesday 4th lay on the floor – it had been there for a *week*. Tomorrow! I was expected to be there – tomorrow . . .

Mr Gowrie was away, he wouldn't be back till the weekend. Once Maisie was settled upstairs doing her homework I found Mrs G and explained that I had to go and I'd be back on the Friday. That part was important during the questioning: 'Did she hear you properly?' 'Did she acknowledge your words?' Sure she did.

"Off you go! I'm here, aren't I?" she said, looking up from her writing. She looked alright, she *seemed* alright that evening. So I went, easy in my mind. I attended the sessions. I spent three nights at the flat.

On Friday evening I came back with a nice farm chicken for supper. I pushed the door open. An unusual quietness met me. Even when things are calm there are sounds at Cleary: the click of Lila's heels on the flagstones, music drifting down from an upstairs room and you'll likely hear the scratch of cat's claws ripping the sofa or the low hum of a left-on computer.

Or maybe its smell tells you when there's living going on? Smoke from a live fire or the damp chalkiness of ashes from the night before. Or food? Even if no one is cooking you can smell where fresh food has been, oatmeal in an unwashed porridge bowl or melting cheese left on the table – or a zesty whiff of coffee, hanging on in the air.

There was nothing.

I paused. I didn't think Lila would have taken Maisie out. Mist was settling on the fields and night dropping fast. I hurried up to the child's room. There were muddy shoes and wet socks on her unmade bed. Her whiteboard was on the floor covered with O's.

At that moment the telephone rang. I ran to get it. A PC Lowry from the police station introduced himself and asked me who I was. I gave my name and described myself as a friend of the family.

"Mrs Gowrie is free to leave," he said.

"What . . ?"

"She's sober now. She can go. Will there be someone at home to receive her."

"Yes, yes – but Maisie? The child? My . . . our . . . I mean *her* daughter? Where is she?"

"The child was given an emergency foster placement last night."

"What . . . ? It's not possible! What are you talking about?"

He said he was not at liberty to discuss the situation. I begged him to tell me where she was. I told him she'd be frightened. I tried to explain she was different; I couldn't find the words . . .

"She'll want to be at home! You *must* let me fetch her back."

"I'm sorry to be the one to tell you, Miss. Cases of neglect are upsetting," he said. "The social worker will be in touch with the parents tomorrow."

"Neglect! There's been a mistake, a terrible mistake. You *must* tell me where . . ."

"Don't shoot the messenger!" he interrupted crossly. "I'm just doing my job. Mr Gowrie has been informed. The lady'll be back shortly. She appears confused."

★　★　★

Twenty minutes later Lila Gowrie arrived in a taxi. I rushed to the door. She was wearing a thin blouse and a rumpled skirt.

"I know," she said, before I could open my mouth.

"What *have* you done now?"

She stood in the doorway shivering, as if she didn't deserve to come into her own house.

"I don't remember. I don't . . ."

I led her into the kitchen and put the kettle on. I put a rug round her shoulders and gave her a cup of tea.

"Neglect!" I said. "The shame of it!"

She stared into space.

"Think back!" I said. "Tuesday? When I was called out? What happened then?"

But she didn't remember a thing. She'd the look of a mad woman and started wandering through a maze of speculation, ever circling back to that wretched son of hers.

"If he hadn't gone this would never have happened."

I tried to get her to focus on Maisie. I begged her to think back. I reminded her that I'd had to leave. I repeated my words to her and her words to me. She'd been writing something. She was alright at the time. I was half way out of it myself, thinking of little Maisie all alone somewhere, sleeping in the wrong bed.

"The shame of it!" I repeated. "I should *never* have left her with you!"

"They told me she was alone for two days," she said, bewildered. "Mrs Scott said she was dirty . . . and hungry. How could that be, Ruth Blane? Her hair wasn't brushed. She didn't have her lunch. They said there was no one in the house. Why weren't we here?"

She was shocked alright, but didn't seem to register her own involvement. It was as if she'd read about it in the paper.

"I'll tell you why. I was at my meetings. Your husband is in Edinburgh. *You were in charge!* If only you'd listen to the messages on your phone. I rang on the Wednesday. Where were you, Mrs G? Did you walk out of that door leaving her? Did you? Did she wake up and come down to this kitchen and not a soul here? Ah, Mary, mother of God . . ."

I'd no restraint, may the Lord forgive me. Maisie isn't like other children, she's as trusting as . . . she's clear as lake water, there's not a ripple on her. She'd have been expecting her porridge.

But when I looked up I wasn't the only one crying. Those dark eyes of hers were filled with tears, a line of eye pencil scribbled its way down her cheek.

"I don't remember," she whispered. "I was in Cork. I was looking for Owen . . ."

Then I knew for a fact that she didn't remember a thing. I felt her grief merge with my grief and fill the room to choking. We looked at each other, helpless. Her hands were lying on the table, palms uppermost. After a while I laid mine on hers.

Later, when I was clearing up, she became frantic all over again.

"Is Maisie missing, Miss Blane? Is she? You haven't told me where she is."

I explained she'd been put with another family for a night or two. I told her that her husband was on his way home and we'd have Maisie back in no time.

But she wasn't taking in a thing I said, raving on making no sense at all. She leaned across the table and asked me if I knew the difference between *missing* and *dead* and, before I could answer, she whispered the word

"Lungs!"

"Lungs? Mrs Gowrie. How's that?"

"When your child is missing it's like losing a lung. You're not dead but part of you is. You breathe in half breaths. I've been half-breathing and half-living for two years."

She smiled wistfully, and for a moment beauty seeped back into her face.

"There used to be days when it was easy to breathe. Air billowing, filling everything, tents, sails, leaves. My baby's clothes flew like little kites on the washing line. My children were here, you see, and my husband – my husband was part of it all. I was a young mother then. No one was missing."

That must have been some bender she was on, I thought to myself. She doesn't know if she's coming or going.

"Cheer up now!" I said. "Maisie will be back in no time. And you know your Flora – she's brave as a lion, you said it yourself. If anyone can find your boy, it'll be her."

★   ★   ★

I wasn't allowed to leave the house until Maisie's case came up. Before this my plan to take her away was fast in my mind, stamped and sealed. I knew the buses and the ferry schedules. Our passports were in order – a mild sedative would be all that was needed. But, watching those two in the days that followed, I began to think things might work themselves out. The child could fall into my hands through circumstance, through divine justice if you like; Edward Gowrie would be needing someone to run things at home. It would be my reward and my due.

Their fear bled like an open wound. The father was sleep-walking, hardly seeing the chair in front of his nose, forgetting to lift the fork to his mouth. And she, like a she-wolf with its last cub gone, was turning in circles, scraping the earth, baying at the moon.

It was clear as day to me that that remaining lung of hers was losing air.

FLORA

I'm getting the hang of things here. It's unreal. Surreal! TTG is a sort of Trinity. You've got three principal beings: There's *their* version of God, a rather backward character who tells them Darwin was wrong and hypes the rib story. And there's the boss of this place, Pathfinder Amos, a divine being according to our moral issues leader. We've only seen him once, being driven off in a Porsche in a pin-striped suit and a cowboy hat. Then their holy ghost is some sort of right-wing philosophy spreading through everything.

There are thirty of us in the girls' initiation building. I had to hand in my iPod and there's no TV. Some of the kids are right into the whole thing, others say lethargically they are here to find themselves. I can't make them out, they don't seem to have done normal things like demonstrating for or against anything.

Every minute of every day is filled. We have lectures on good and evil, meditation, chanting, robust hymns, two hours of physical labour, reflection periods and films – not normal films like *Pretty Woman* or *Star-Trek*. Turn To God helps deprived people in some African countries. The films we get are about grateful natives on remote islands. They've been issued with TTG T-shirts and grey packets of porridge. The shirts look gross over their beautiful dark skin and don't go with tie-dyed, swirling skirts. The women look sad, as if they'd rather be dancing to their own gods and eating delicious yams and things they've grown themselves.

Yesterday we were talking about the war in Afghanistan. 'What about civilian deaths?' I asked. There was silence, then the lecturer said: 'Didn't I know that women could be rebels too?

Didn't I know that underneath their Burkas they could be carrying guns? I should learn to leave that sort of question up to our great leader,' she said in a reverent voice.

There is also compulsory one-to-one psychological counselling. My psychologist is an elderly hippie with long hair, seed beads and a floor-length skirt. Her name is Janie Gospel. It was in a session with her that I made my first mistake. I told her about Owen and asked her for help. I thought she'd be delighted to hear I might have a brother in the organization – how wrong was that?

"It would be impossible for me to identify your brother if he was here," she said, looking at me suspiciously. "Our members are renamed as they commit to their new family."

"I could describe him," I said hopefully. "Fair hair, lanky, good looking by most girls' standards, about six foot two, never ties his laces . . ."

"Marina," she said, using my new name in her flat, deadly serious voice. "You have been graciously accepted into our introductory guest quarters. Only Pathfinder Amos and our senior leaders have access to birth names. Besides, you will have no need for a brother here. TTG *is* your family."

She smiles and nods in a maddening way when she says the word *family*.

"It is our father and mother, our nurturer and friend." I could see where this was going.

"Gee, that's great," I said, humbly. "I'm lonesome for a real family."

It staved her off. She gave me an uncomfortable lesbian hug. She smelled sickly sweet, of some animal extract and cactus massage oils. YUK!

"That's what we're here for, honey."

* * *

I wasn't working out as a spy. I needed help. I was hungry and homesick and couldn't sleep for wanting Patrick. I'd been noticing a beautiful black girl in our dormitory called Imogene. She didn't fit. She had a lovely singing voice. I guessed it was because she was a natural, not because she was into the hymns. She looked scornful during lectures and wore *Victoria's Secret* knickers and bras under her TTG T-shirt and shorts. I decided to risk it.

"How come you're here?" I asked her one night after prayers.

"It's to get me off of something, babe. My daddy sent me here because I'd developed a bad-ass habit!"

"Is it working?" I asked her. "I mean this place."

"You know, I'm trying to re-spect these clowns, Marina honey, I really am, but it's hard. They are just so stu-pid."

"Flora." I whispered. "I'm Flora, not Marina. I'm on a mission."

So we made friends, real friends. We'd sneak outside in the warm nights after the electricity was switched off. I'd arrived in an air-conditioned taxi so I hadn't realized how hot and isolated the place is. It sings with heat all day and hardly cools off at night. The desert is white under the moon. Clumps of tufty, dry grasses stretch for miles before you see the outline of forbidding mountains with Indian names. We would lie on the sandy ground, talking. I told her about Owen, about how I sensed he was here somewhere but couldn't prove it. I told her about Alan Corvin back at the motel and a bit about Patrick, a fair bit about him. I said I thought Janie Gospel might be onto me.

"Yeah?" she said. "Now you be real careful, babe. You wanna watch out for yourself. Just let me do some hard, ha-rd thinking.

Watch out for myself? The place was beautiful in its way – the sky was bigger and bolder than at home. Vivid flowers sprang out of shrivelled cacti and, despite the endless shimmer of heat; you could hear the sound of falling water in the distance. There were no shops or bars or Indians handing out love potions. The only sign of life was the desert animals. They lived mainly underground, as if the daytime glare was too much for them, but at night you could see dear little brown faces poking out of holes, checking that the coast was clear to play and hunt in the moonlight.

A week later we were outside again. It was my sixteenth birthday and I was feeling miserable about not getting any presents and desperate about Owen. I hadn't managed to get a thing on Cristina, either . . . how can you possibly find people when their very names have been stolen? Their true selves and souls must have evaporated by now, absorbed into rock and sand.

"Now you re-lax," Imogene said gently.

She rolled a joint. I tried a puff or two, the sky was chock-full of stars, the same stars that must be shining on Ireland. They crowded together and lit up every stone, but nothing changed.

"Listen, Flora! I think I can help. Remember you were asking about the other kids? Well I figure they all have something in common."

"Oh?"

"Yeah! If they aren't holy they're rich, or their daddies are rich, and when they are rich it's like *very* rich. I'll bet you could buy that brother of yours right out of this outfit."

"But this is a religious set up . . ."

"You are one naïve kid," Imogene said. "Ever notice the parts we don't get? There ain't no Good Samaritans round here. They aren't pushing the widow's mite, are they now? TTG's god is one rich god, honey, with the Dow Jones average on his mind."

"But Imogene, I don't have any money. And why are you here if you know all this bad stuff?"

"I came here to try to get good again, but it ain't working. There's nothing they've got that isn't right here in ma very own heart."

I tried another puff. It was really great being sixteen after all – as good as a present. It would impress Patrick enormously! It would make him want to kiss me again – and again. I thought about that and felt better, flying in fact, as if I was a desert star in the heavens, blinking on and off with all the others. Then I thought about God and remembered what Imogene had said about TTG's god loving money . . .

"Hey, you've given me an idea, darling," I said. "Thanks!"

★ ★ ★

"Oh, Janie," I said at my next one-on-one. "I've been so looking forward to this session."

"Why, Marina, I prayed for a change of heart."

"The only reason I was on about my brother was because of the money . . ."

"Money? What money is that? Would that be money that belongs to your brother?"

Her oily skin took on a slight gleam, a flicker of interest showed in her washed-out 60's eyes.

"Sort of. I mean how to give him his share? I need him for signing stuff. Our parents would have wanted . . ."

I made a choking sound, a 'huuh, huh hu-u' sound I'd been practicing.

". . . and now that I see all the great things you do."

"Your parents have passed on, honey?"

"The accident! He doesn't even *know* . . ."

I'm good at bringing tears to my eyes. You just say, 't'babydied t'babydied t'babydied' over and over and out they come.

Janie Gospel handed me a tissue. "You poor child!"

"You see, Owen's the one who guides me. I need to find him because he'll know what to do . . ."

I made a shorter huuh, hu-h, sound,

"about the London house and stuff."

"Of course you need to see your brother," she said, wrapping a caftan-clad arm around me. "You did right to tell me, Marina. I appreciate your coming to me – to us – to your new family. I'll see what I can do."

She left the room with a slight skip in her usual meditative, sleepy walk. "Now, you just hold on."

It was a cinch really, easier than winning over Warren-Barnes, easier than leaving Maisie . . .

★   ★   ★

Do be patient. As trust is established the cult member will be prone to share some of his misgivings.
Do allow your cult member to express positive feelings about the cult and other cult members.
Don't pressure the cult member to voice his doubts.

I could feel my heart beating, tight under my ribs. I recited the bits I'd memorized again. I'd been put in a room with stacked chairs along one side and an empty podium at the end. I kept my eye on the stage – it seemed the most likely place for Owen to appear, striding in like Hamlet – a TTG soliloquy on his lips.

Do be patient. As trust is established . . .

I felt, rather than saw, a presence in the room behind me. I turned round slowly. It was Owen, or rather a skeleton of Owen.

Thin-faced, older-looking, shaven-headed, totally unlike himself. He was wearing a white tunic, like the leaders.

"Flora! Is that you? Flo! I hardly recognise you . . ."

The *how to approach your loved one* rules went flying out of my head.

"Owen! *What are you doing here?* Are you mad? Look at you! You freaky, barefoot, disappeared . . . maniac!"

He stood silently, staring at me.

"I've been practising the rules of how to treat you." I said. "That wasn't it."

"Have you come all this way to find me, Flo?"

"What d'you think, Owen? Sure! I'm in Arizona by chance, just passing . . ."

"Oh, dear! Oh, no – you shouldn't have come. You mustn't stay here. I can't leave, you know."

"You mean because the outside world is an imperfect place? Is that it? It's what you think, right? While this haven of fucked-up misfits breaking doughnuts together and going to sleep to a brotherhood/sisterhood tape is the answer to . . ."

"Don't do this, please."

He stretched out his arms. I stayed where I was. They dropped back to his side.

"How are they, Flo? Ma and Dad?"

I asked him how *he* thought they were? I told him how they try to believe he's not dead every single day. I spelled it out for him: the quarrels, Ma's drinking, Dad combing the world to find him. I told him he didn't deserve to know . . .

"It's true. I've no right to ask – but Maisie?" he said her name softly. "Please, please tell me . . ."

His eyes pled with mine. I looked at him carefully. He sounded strange. He wasn't speaking properly.

"Maisie thinks you are Jesus, Owen. She talks to you all the time. Haven't you been listening? She doesn't realize you're a fraud, an attention-seeking Houdini who hasn't had the balls to make a telephone call to his mother for two years."

He started to talk then, in short robotic sentences. I couldn't catch it all.

"It's a sacred trust, Flora. Secrecy is an important part, part of the philosophy. I trusted them, you see. I thought they had the answer. To questions. Overwhelming questions. I put my trust in their hands. In God's hands. Overwhelming . . . questions. We, some people that is, can't stop searching. We are looking, searching . . . I was seduced into the TTG way of thinking.

"That's not all that seduced you," I couldn't resist saying.

"No, no it isn't. I loved her, the woman you saw that time. I believed I loved her. I didn't know then that sex is part of the recruitment strategy."

He looked so desolate I couldn't go on attacking him. I explained how I'd managed to find him. I told him about Mr Warren-Barnes and Cristina and about Alan getting me into the initiation quarters. I boasted a little when it came to my trick with Janie Gospel. I told him Alan was at the motel and warned him to be ready to be rescued . . .

Owen seemed appalled by what I was saying. He kept looking round anxiously. He moved closer to me and interrupted, talking in a rush of urgent words. He kept repeating the word *dangerous*. There was something physically wrong with him, I was sure of it. He seemed unsteady on his legs. He was hanging onto the back of a chair.

"I can't leave, Flora," he said. "I saw it happening. They know I saw . . ."

"Saw *what* happening?"

"There are children here. I can't leave them now."

That set me off again.

"Oh yeah? But you can leave your family, right? We don't matter. We happen to have a child too. Isn't Maisie a child? Our little sister, remember her? Our parents are pretty cool, Owen. They can take a lot of weird stuff, but they aren't good at *nothing* – knowing *nothing*."

While I was raging on Owen loosened his grasp on the chair and began to slip to the floor. I grabbed him round the waist.

"Owen, I'm sorry! Dear Owen, get up! Please, please get up!"

I helped him onto the chair. His white dead-looking feet stuck out of his tunic. His elbows were like chicken wings. He was begging me to leave before anyone came, when suddenly the door opened and two TTG leaders burst in. They rushed over to us and began pulling me off my brother. I hung onto him for dear life, kicking and biting. The last thing I remember is a sharp acid smell and having something rubbery thrust into my mouth.

MAISIE

Would you believe it, Owen, I woke up and no one was in! Not Flo, not Ma, not Dad, not Miss Blane, – you weren't in your room either. I didn't mind. I did my usual every morning things. For breakfast I ate a bowl of cereal without milk. It was lovely. I skipped on the way to school.

When I got home after my classes it was the same again. Nobody here. And no tea! The house was quiet. I did my homework like always, Then I played hopscotch in the garden. Then I was hungry for supper. I ate 3 whole apples, every bit of them, except the stalk. I was still hungry so I stood on a chair and reached for the biscuit tin; It slipped and fell. The biscuits broke into pieces. I left the dusty parts and ate the big bits from the top of the pile.

That whole night there was nobody here. I had my bath and said my prayers and fell asleep like always but, in the morning, another day came with no one here. It was weird!. I dressed in Wednesday's clothes. I put my red party shoes on, because my school ones weren't there. When I got downstairs the cats were all over the place, mewing and rubbing up against me. I couldn't open their food tin. They went on mewing and mewing . . . so I gave them a nice salmon from the freezer. They tore round, licking and biting at it.

On the way to school I was cold. I felt scratchy and funny-looking. I thought about the lilies of the field in the Jesus stories and considered them like He said. After a bit I stopped minding about my clothes. I knew Jesus would have an eye out for me – and the cats. At lunchtime I was very very very hungry, Owen. I looked at the other kids' food. Annie Roberts saw me looking. She broke her baguette in two and handed me the biggest half. It had lettuce and cheese and bacon and mayonnaise in it.

I love Annie. I love her kind face. I wanted to say thank you and to tell her about me being alone. The words were pushing to be said, but I don't talk at school, do I? I can't. So I gave her a kiss and ate it.

In the afternoon I was sent to Mrs Scott's office. She looked at my hair and my party shoes and the mud on my skirt. She was cross. She spoke on the telephone tat tater tat. *I sat in a chair thinking about the way Annie had given me half of her lunch – just like that. Two new ladies came into the office with talk and questions tipping out of their mouths. They asked me about Ma and Flo and Miss Blane. I didn't answer.*

Now I'm in a strange place, Owen. It's not a proper house. There's a man and a lady and three children in a blue room with a loud television. The sofa is slippery. You can see it's a sofa for the cover is clear but it's cold on your legs, not the sort to let you curl up. There's a silver Christmas tree in the room, although it isn't Christmas and the tree's not a real tree. I touched the branches. They felt like hard shiny fur. There's a present under the tree wrapped in dusty Christmas paper. I don't think the present is real either. I don't have my things with me, Owen. I don't have my colours. The fat lady gave me a new toothbrush and pyjamas. They are boy's pyjamas. I won't wear them.

I want to go home now. Ma will be after fetching me soon, isn't that right? She'll be on her way, for sure. She will, won't she, Owen?

CHAPTER
8

MISS BLANE

We were outside the family courtroom, the four of us – waiting. Lila Gowrie had somehow got herself together. She was dressed for battle, wearing a leopard-skin jacket with a wide leather belt, sheer stockings and Gucci boots. Maisie was sitting on her daddy's knee playing cat's cradle, being coached by her mother.

"Maisie! Now listen to me! There's a roomful of creeps in there and you've got to say what *they* want to hear. You've got to, darling, because you want to come home now, don't you?"

Maisie looked gravely at her mother.

"It's important! You have to break your rules, just for once. Think of this place as the kitchen at home. Maisie! Are you listening? Think of the stove. Think of Lorca lying on it and the way his tail hangs down like a furry rope. Think of the snorting kettle. Remember how warm it is . . .

Pretend you're *there*, darling – not *here*. It's easy speaking there, isn't it? You must tell them you want to come home. They're so thick . . . I mean they are not very clever at understanding what people really want – so it's up to you. I'm afraid that means talking – *Words!*"

"Easy, Lila!" her husband said. "She'll try to tell them, won't you, my little love? Then we can all go home . . ."

"The thing is, Maisie, they're such fuc . . . such poor, silly ladies, they have to be told that you love us. We don't mind about words at home, do we? But if you could toss out a few to keep them happy . . . Miss Blane can wait outside if you feel better without her."

"Lila!"

"Flo will be back soon, Maisie. You wouldn't want to miss . . ."

There was a knock at the door. We were invited to follow a woman who I recognized slightly from the Centre. Lila gave me a jab in the ribs with one gloved hand to indicate that I should stay behind.

"All of you, please!" the woman said firmly.

We sat round a large table. There were the four of them: Mrs McKinley, the foster parent; Mrs Scott, Maisie's headmistress; Brian Fitzgerald, the school social worker and a gaunt woman, with a grey chignon and heavy metal spectacles, who they called Dr Gail. You could almost hear the prayers in our hearts. It had been six long days without her – six.

★ ★ ★

In the courtroom they were informal and friendly at first, acting like a little girl's future wasn't at stake. But soon enough the questions began, and then they came thick and fast.

Dr Gail began by asking the foster mother how Maisie had reacted to her new situation and how she got on with the other children. The woman was not one to answer a question directly. We had to listen to a long list of her successes, remedies, baking tips and the birthday treats she provided. 'Tere's not a child doesn't come round to Milly McKinley,' she kept repeating, her double chins wobbling over her blouse, her sagging bosoms wobbling over a pair of pink, synthetic trousers you'd not have caught me wearing to the rubbish tip.

After closer questioning, she admitted the child didn't speak much.

"Much?" the doctor asked.

"She'd have come round in no time."

"Did she speak or did she not speak?"

"She did not," the McKinley woman said sulkily, "'tere was stubbornness about her . . ."

"That will be all," she was told.

When Edward Gowrie's turn came he spoke slowly, making sure to include everyone. He said Maisie had been alone because of an unprecedented misunderstanding, taking most of the blame on himself. He explained, in terms that would move the hardest heart, what his wife had gone through. She was now a member of AA, he told the group, bravely confronting her problem. (Anonymous with a capital A, I'd say! It was news to me.) He added that I had been employed to give Maisie stability and professional help.

Lila Gowrie played the *poor me* act to the hilt: "I had understood she was in charge," she said, pitifully, pointing at me. "You have to trust someone in this life . . . I let Ruth Blane stay occasionally because, as anyone can see, she's a lonely old woman. Despite her obvious failings," she went on, "she'd proved reliable up until then." At this point she paused for a shower of pretty tears. "How could I have known that she'd let me down on that fateful evening?"

Lies! Wicked lies, but I'd the sense to ignore her outrageous story and answered the questions put to me with quiet authority. Mr Fitzgerald did his best to put me on the spot. "How much did Maisie talk at home? How would I rate my communication with the child? And the mother?" I told him I had an excellent relationship with both. I took care *not* to cast blame where blame is due, for don't I know how these people work? One slip and you're done for. Finally, Mrs Scott turned to Maisie.

"Maisie Gowrie! You're a big girl now and I'm sure you'd like to help us. You've been with the kind McKinley family these past days and settled down nicely. Now, we know your poor mummy hasn't been well and your sister and brother are not at home. It must be lonely for you without them, dear?"

Maisie gave her an abstracted glance, She was rumpling the fur on her mother's jacket and stroking it smooth, as if it was a kitten.

"Pay attention, please, Maisie! We need to know if you would like to stay with Mrs McKinley with the nice trampoline in Pine Tree Avenue – or if you'd prefer to go back to your parent's house?"

There was silence for a full minute that had my heart stopping in its tracks.

"Well?" she repeated. "Where would you like to live?"

Maisie looked the woman straight in the eyes and smiled.

"Sure and my mother warned me you'd need it explained like they do at school," she started off. "Isn't that something? I've to get back home now for Ma wants me at my piano lessons and Dad hasn't a soul to play with when I'm away and Miss Blane'll be missing me. She has a great love for sounds and letters – she's a mother too, you see, but not so pretty."

There was laughter all round. It was the first time I'd heard her say my name in her light musical voice – *a mother!* I was delighted. Mothers have no right to be pretty in my book – a lot of good it does them.

"So you don't want to stay with the kind McKinleys, Maisie?"

"What would I be doing there? I've Lorca and the little cats waiting on me and my sister and brother back any moment now . . ."

And that was that. She wouldn't answer another thing and

they had to agree she should go home. As soon as it broke up the Gowrie's were off with Maisie, down some back steps into a waiting taxi, without a thought for me.

But I had my moment! It was me got my picture in the *Examiner*. There I am on page four in my light blue suit and my dark blue pillbox hat answering questions. Now I know how the stars feel, poised on a top step with the flash of cameras below. "Yes, I'm like a family member!" I told them, 'Yes, I was described by the child as a second mother!' Then a man asked: "Was it true that Mrs Gowrie was in Murphy's bar while her little girl walked to school alone?" I thought for a minute and said: "No comment." And when a cheeky lad spoke up and said he'd heard the girl was a mute I told him to wash his mouth out and was raising my bag to give him a whack when a policeman came and escorted me to my bus stop.

★   ★   ★

I was due an apology from Lila Gowrie for her behaviour at the meeting, a tribute to my loyalty at the very least. But once she'd read the papers the next morning, she was after me with all the old venom, just as if we'd never shared our trouble, holding hands at the kitchen table.

"What did you mean by saying 'No comment' when they asked if I was in Murphy's bar while my child went to school alone?" she asked, waving a cigarette threateningly in my face.

"Would you rather I'd said *yes?*"

"*Mujer, imposible!*" she exclaimed, striking her forehead. "I'd rather you just bugger off and keep your nose out of our business."

I don't hear her. I don't listen anymore. I'll stay on for now to settle Maisie, then I've business to attend to, a journey she knows nothing about.

★ ★ ★

One of those evenings, when Maisie was in care, I went to the bay for the first time in my life. As I climbed down the rock steps I could see two dots in the distance. They vanished into a wave, reappeared and were lost again in a slate sky. The trawlers finally arrived in the port with a stuttering chug, making a wooden thud as they banged up against the pier. There were shouts, curses and laughter. *The stink of the fishermen* Mother had said so often, but it wasn't a stink to me . . . the smell was strangely nostalgic, as if I'd known it all my life. The men smelled of wind and sun and the fresh silvery fish that were flying through the air as they tossed them into pails.

It occurred to me, slowly at first, that one absent father was not the same as another. For wasn't Mr Blane a myth of my mother's making? She'd invented a father to please herself and tried to make me hate the one she'd taken away. I got to thinking about this father of mine, just off a boat, strong and young like these boys. It would have been June, early in the month. Nine months counted backwards is not hard. A Nordic man, Aunt Minna said. Perhaps Eileen could trace him on her computer.

I could have a father, a real one! And this father of mine might *want* a daughter. At least he'd be disposed to like her, its nature, isn't it? I've seen them on television, fathers finding daughters, weeping for joy. My father . . . well, he might own a fishery by now? Or he could be running cruises up and down those fjords? Or he could be a ship-owner? That *would* be status . . .

I'd been mad to think of kidnapping Maisie. Why go against the law when it's there, to serve you? When you have right on your side? I'm the one with the qualities they're after: a loving mother-figure with no criminal record would put a hysterical, negligent, alcoholic birth-mother in the shade – and a ship-owning grandfather? Well, they could hardly turn us down!

★ ★ ★

That night in my room I took another look at the *Examiner*. I will say the photo's nice, I'd had time to put my make-up to rights and my hair's neat. My navy scarf's blowing in the wind like Isadora Duncan's and Mother's patent leather shoes would not look amiss on the queen of England. I'm centre stage! Right there in my fine suit. I look like I've been giving interviews to the press all my life.

There's nothing to be ashamed of in that photograph, not a thing that wouldn't make a father proud.

FLORA

I woke up on a narrow bed in a small room. There were bars on the window and a sliding panel on the door like a real prison. A cubicle with a shower and a loo led off the room. I was cool at first. I did things prisoners in books do, checked for a loose bar on the window, looked for an air conditioner with a removable frame and tapped the walls to find out if there were fellow sufferers to communicate with. Nobody tapped back.

Then I realized this bloody well *was* an emergency. It was time to signal Alan. I felt for the tiny machine he'd given me which nestled in my left groin supported by an invisible wire that went round my waist. When he'd showed me how it worked, I remember saying. "You'd think I was going to poison a president!' 'You might need it," he'd replied calmly. "Why don't you shove it up my bum?" I'd suggested cheekily. "No need to go that far," he'd said. "Take it kid, you never know." I ran my fingers round my waist and felt up my back. The wire had gone.

At that point I'm ashamed to say I freaked. A lump of fear in my chest made it hard to breathe. I kicked the door, screaming and swearing till my toes hurt. I pulled the headboard off the bed and tried to break the window by prodding it through the bars. When nothing worked I threw myself on the floor and sobbed like a baby.

That evening a lady doctor came to examine me. She was accompanied by a pale, frightened-looking Janie Gospel who stood close to the door, nervously biting her fingernails, ready to make a break for it if I got violent. The doctor felt me down – and up – for hidden weapons and treated my bruised knuckles.

"We are troubled by your behaviour, Marina." Janie said. "We have reason to believe you are not who you say you are. Pathfinder Amos is away this week. You will have time to reflect and repent before he looks into your case."

She rushed her words, then tapped a series of coded taps on the door. It opened – and they fled.

Days! In this room. After another bout of crying, I got my act together and thought it over. I decided to fast. It's a strategy that gets a lot of attention in Ireland. Dad says they hardly ever let the person die.

That night, when they pushed my dinner through the sliding panel, I pushed it back. I heard the tray fall and the plates smash on the other side. It was satisfying, but the smell reached me. It was roast chicken and chips. I imagined the chicken's golden breast lying tragically in the dust, my mouth remembered the crunch of chips, the way your teeth hit crispy potato skin then follow through into the buttery inside. There was a lemony whiff too, and a fluffy whiff of something sugary. It might have been lemon meringue pie.

Lunch the next day was harder. I was famished. I looked, before I shoved. It was spaghetti with Bolognese sauce. On top of the sauce was a golden tower of grated parmesan cheese. There was half an avocado and a cupcake. I heard the plates smash. Everything must be jumbled up: the avocado squashed into the cake, chocolate bits floating in the meat sauce . . . later I heard the swish of a mop as someone cleaned it up.

No one spoke to me. No one came begging me to eat.

At lunchtime on the third day I broke my fast. Obviously they weren't sophisticated enough for fasts in America. Lunch was wonderful – a cheeseburger, baked potato, salad and peach ice-cream.

But, after the glow of the food had worn off, I felt sadder than ever. I am not into praying but I fell back on it. I prayed to the real God, who obviously has nothing to do with TTG. I bet He is dead against gloom and confessions to fallible priests. I imagine Him loving the way Imogene sings: *Were you there when they crucified my Lord?* He probably spends lots of time watching His creation. It must be one long movie for Him, with bits that make Him proud and bits, like elephant poachers and people who tip rubbish into His rivers, that make Him want to give up altogether.

I'm sure He's looking down on all of us – especially people in need, like Owen. I psyched myself into a spiritual mode and waited. I waited . . . and waited. Gradually, an image of Jesus' gentle, listening face came into focus. He was here! In this room, close to me . . .

I begged Him to get us out of TTG. I remembered Cristina and added her into my prayer. I felt His love for me, like warmth on my skin, like a slow sun. I closed my eyes and felt His breath on my eyelids and the palm of His hand on my forehead. After that I stopped asking for things because I realized that I didn't have to explain what they've done or tell Him how frightened I was, because He knows – everything.

What actually happened in the end wasn't mysterious at all. God hit on the obvious answer. He worked through Imogene, who is probably an angel anyway. She was the only person who knew where Alan Corvin and the Warren-Barnes parents were and all about me being a spy. I'd told her about Janie Gospel and we'd laughed about the money. When I didn't turn up on the second day she guessed I might have been taken to meet Owen and was in some kind of trouble.

The following night she waited till everyone was asleep then set off to get help. At the TTG gate there's a guard with a gun and a Rottweiler. Imogene found another way out. She walked five and a half miles to the motel where Cristina's parents and

Alan Corvin were staying. She followed dry river beds, keeping as close as she could to the hum of the highway. Her feet and ankles were scratched by rocks and her red shoes were done for. When Alan heard her story he called the police immediately.

I was fast asleep when the screech of police cars and the sound of boots loud on the tiles woke me. My door was shattered with a kick. I was hauled out of bed, rushed outside and pushed into the back of a van. When my eyes got used to the dark I saw Owen, hunched in the far corner. We were driven at top speed to the motel.

Alan Corvin came out to meet us; he pushed a path through a flash of lights as journalists took pictures of us arriving, dazed and frightened in our pyjamas. Inside the café was bright and cold. I was standing alone still shaking when Imogene came running up and put her arms around me. She was looking lovely, wearing white flowing trousers, a camisole and a pair of new sparkly high-heeled shoes on her narrow black feet.

She took me to a table and ordered some tea. "What happened? How did you manage it?" I asked, after we'd hugged each other and I'd calmed down.

"It was hard, Flora honey, you know how ah shake when 'ah even thinks of a snake or a spider, but those river beds were guidin' paths in the starlight. I was led by the hand; there ain't no doubt about that."

"But Imogene, what will you do now? Where will you go?"

"Well, one thing I do know is ah'm not going back to that no-good, godless place, never! And ah'm not going to that mean daddy of mine, neither." She smiled her slow, sweet smile and poured me another cup of tea.

"But, but how can I leave you?"

"Look at your brother, girl. Jus' look!"

He was sitting on a sofa with a blanket round his shoulders.

Alan was talking quietly to him. Even from across the room we could hear the lift and fall of Alan's voice, like a parent comforting a small child.

"You've gotta get that boy home – and you've gotta get back to that beau of yours, sweetheart. Patience ain't a quality that frequents the male sex, not even the good ones."

"But . . ."

"Don't you worry about me, Flora. I've got songs in ma head and places to sing at and, thanks to you, ah'm feeling free as a lark!"

★ ★ ★

MAISIE

Everything's still here. I'm checking, Owen. My school shoes are in the cupboard. My blue nighty is under my pillow. The white ones are in the airing cupboard folded and warm, like always. My colours are sharpened with their points looking upwards, like always. Purple is missing, but purple was missing before. Before . . . before I was there, I mean, not here – there. . . in the other house.

Dad says it was because of a big mistake. Ma says I'm not going anywhere – ever again. I don't want to go anywhere. Ma slept on the put-up bed beside me for three nights. It was funny her being so near. She kept reaching across my bed in the middle of the night. I felt her patting my quilt, feeling for me, when she found a bit of me she took her hand away and went to sleep again – then her hand came back, patting and finding. Once her whole arm reached across me and stayed there. It felt heavy and safe.

Lorca is on my chair making his dark purr, like always. The hot tap's the same as always, too hot to touch, wanting a flannel round it when you turn it on. I'm checking. I have the flannel here.

Marion hee-hawed when she saw me. She needed scratching along her back, and apples. I kissed the sore place on her neck and combed her mane.

In the kitchen there are new biscuits in the tin, Owen, lots and lots of them. Miss Blane says she'll get the tin down for me any time, I only have to ask. She keeps on smiling. When I skip she skips too. She brushes my hair when it's brushed already. She whistles and hums. I'm playing the piano with Ma again and beating Dad at Pelmanism, like always.

I was hardly scared at all, Owen.

Well, only sometimes.

Just a little . . .
These are happy tears, not sad ones.
I'm home . . .
Hooray!

CHAPTER
9

MISS BLANE

You can have abroad, that's what I say!

Hours! I was all night on the bus, up and down those fiords like a switchback, not an ounce of flat to be seen. There was a lady from Galway on the trip and we got chatting. She was on her way to visit elderly parents. 'Did I have any children?' she wanted to know. I told her I had a girl of eight, a credit to me, top of her class! She asked me where I was going. I said my dad was getting on and wasn't happy if he didn't see me every year. She got out at a pretty resort town. Then we were off again; up, up into woods with enormous gloomy trees blocking out the sun and lumps of left-over snow messing up the ground.

Finally we arrived at Fjellaasen. Sure and I didn't expect a palace but the village was all wood and smoke. Though I'm not one to look down on anyone, the people looked like peasants. Still, it was a father I was after, a real relative; I had the address in my hand.

I asked the way and got not a word of English back. Wouldn't you think they'd learn to speak properly at the school? Finally a child indicated I should follow him. It was close on a mile with me tripping along in my best shoes, dragging my new case over stones. Then the road vanished and the lad sped up such a steep track I'd to carry the case for fear the wheels would fall off.

He lives in a cabin, there's no better way of putting it. I found him at half ten in the morning fixing a dismantled gun, with a bottle of clear alcohol in front of him. He looked up when I came in. There was no doubt it was my father for wasn't I looking in the glass? He'd a broad brow like mine and the same generous nose. Recognition, strong as a north wind, fairly knocked the air out of my lungs.

He stared at me.

"Father!"

I don't know what I'd expected but nothing happened. I touched my face and pointed at his.

"Father? Papa? . . . Dad?" As I said the words tears started to flow, mine not his. They'd been storing up all my life. There was no stopping them.

"I am your daughter," I said when I could speak, flushing, still out of breath from the walk.

By now he was looking worried. Suddenly I remembered the photograph. I took it out of my bag and gave it to him. In it Mother is sitting in a café looking smart as smart in a beige suit with a light cardigan thrown over her shoulders. Her hair is long and loose. I never saw it long. I never saw it loose.

It had a dramatic effect. He let out a voluble sigh and traced the image of her face with his finger. He looked at me again and shouted instructions to the child who was still in the doorway. In a minute the boy was back with a neighbour called Olda who spoke English. Another stream of words followed. The woman looked at me shyly.

"He wants me to ask if you are the girl of Weenifred of many years ago in Ireland."

"I am."

"Nei! Nei, Nei . . ." Even I could follow that. He poured himself a glass of the transparent liquor and words came flooding out of his mouth as he shook his head repeatedly.

"What's he saying?"

She looked embarrassed. "He is saying he has enough childrens already and that childrens have more childrens and he is a simple man with many problems and all he wants is peace."

"Si till henne at hun man dra hjemm!"

"What does that mean?"

"It is not so nice," Olda said, awkwardly.

"Please!"

"It means: 'Tell her to go home!'" she admitted, handing me a clean cotton handkerchief and taking my case from me. "Pay no attention to Olaf. He's old and has no one to care for him. Maybe he will change. You come to my house, thank you! Later he may be happy."

He trilled out another question, pointing at me, smiling for the first time in a macabre way.

She gave him a trilling right back. He repeated his question.

"He wants to know if you have presents in that case – a bottle of Irish whiskey, perhaps?"

I let him have it then.

"Miles! Tell him I've been travelling two days to find him. Tell him I came looking for my father, for affection's sake, to help him, to be a daughter. Yes! I do have presents in this case, though he'll not get a bottle of whiskey off me. Tell him I'm here because he's the one that made me, because his blood runs in my veins, for sweet Jesus' sake."

She translated all this. It took a long time. He sunk his head in his hands.

★ ★ ★

Olda had a far nicer house with a big tiled stove, a large bath and a sauna. While I was bathing she prepared food for the three of us. I don't mind telling you that what we sat down to is not what I call a meal – there were squares of black bread with bits of wilting fish, hard cheese and fish eggs. For pudding there was a tub of yoghurt with an odd taste.

"From sheeps!" Olda said proudly. I hadn't the heart to tell her the ones at home are better.

Two days passed and we were not getting on at all. My father wouldn't look at me. He even stopped communicating through Olda.

Then I heard that a daughter of his, Sonia, with four children, was about to appear. *Soster* is the Norwegian word for sister. I loved it, soon as I heard it. It hadn't crossed my mind that I might have a sister. Only think! I could be an aunt, with three nephews, a niece and a *sister* in my life. We'd have a visit planned and little gifts between us. I'd be getting a pattern and cutting out a dress for the *datter*, Haaken. I'd be sending the baby proper Irish toys. That would be *family*, and not a one of them missing. Lila Gowrie could put that in her pipe and smoke it!

When she first heard who I was Sonia gave me a kiss on both cheeks. My hopes rose. She talked quite good English but soon enough I was getting an earful of her woes. How could she work with four kids? There was day care in Norway but she wasn't eligible for it. The baby was sick . . . would I help her? I would, I did. I had little Olaf with his ash blond hair shampooed, his clothes washed and a meal of porridge in him in no time.

I put off my return for eight days caring for those children like they were my own. But, before long, I got a better picture of this *soster* of mine. She was little more than a tramp. 'Could I lend her some *penger*, just for a month?' You didn't have to be a linguist to know what *penger* meant as she rubbed her thumb over her fingers and turned her purse upside down. She wanted me settled in her cabin, a wreck worse than our father's, doing the work while she was off with her latest fellow. There were several of them sniffing round after her: big, blond, hairy creatures in leather jackets with Motor-bikes.

One night there was a fight between two of them. Olda explained that the alcohol they drink is called *hjemmebrent*, which means 'home burned.' My first evening I'd tried it out of politeness. It burned alright! It scorched my stomach and had me half out of my wits. My sister was in the habit of taking it disguised in coffee and, after a few of those coffees, she'd be off on the back of one of the bikes, skirt riding up to her knickers, thick plaits flying, leaving me with four hungry children.

You can't pull the wool over my eyes. I've seen her kind before. I was sorry to leave the kids, but I had a life of my own and Maisie would be missing me.

★ ★ ★

As the bus hurtled back to Bergen I was overcome with shame, the failure of it. I'd no father, no mother, no sister, no baby – no one loving *me* . . . the hurt built up and up and up and had me weeping into my hanky and then my scarf. I couldn't stop. By the time we reached the coast, my hurt turned to anger, broke and curdled like milk in a pan. How was it I never got a chance? Fourteen years old with pins never out of my mouth and never a cuddle? Now my father'd turned out as cold and as mean as street ice. Nothing! Nothing, from him, not a question, not a family story, not a laugh, no kind old hand patting mine . . .

On the ferry I dabbed my eyes and scrubbed my face. Nothing would stop me this time. I'd have no mercy. I'd tell them the truth about Lila Gowrie. Then and there I started the first draft of a long overdue report. I'd get my girl. It would change my life forever and, for certain sure, it would finish off her's.

I have been working with Maisie Grace Gowrie since August 2011 and regret to say I have certain disturbing matters to disclose.

During the unfortunate episode in which the child was given a temporary foster placement on April 9th, followed by a family out-of-court meeting on April 16th, certain truths were suppressed.

Maisie Gowrie's birth-mother, Lila Garcia-Gowrie, is an alcoholic. She has never been a member of AA and shows no interest in solving her drinking problem. It was due to an alcohol-induced state on April 7th that the her daughter found herself alone in Cleary Court and spent a day and two nights alone before her situation was brought to Mrs Scott's attention . . .

I went on, sketching out their downfall. Explaining the situation with nothing spared.

Missing son
Drunken scenes in front of the girls
Flora leaving home at 15
LG's worsening condition
Gross negligence when LG abandoned the child
Emergency foster care
Adverse effect on the child

As the only responsible, loving figure in Maisie Grace Gowrie's life I would like to put forward a possible solution for your consideration. Through personal contact I have

formed an interest in and fondness for this child. My affection for her is reciprocated.

I would like to ask the team involved in her case to consider me as a possible foster parent for Maisie Grace Gowrie.

⋆　⋆　⋆

I worked on it for a week in the flat before returning to Cleary Court. I read up on the latest fostering laws, theories and recommendations. I dwelt on my suitability and recent inheritance.

For the borrow of my best blouse and a fair sum of money, Eileen O'Hanson helped me with the research and difficult words like *suppress* and *thus*.

When I got back to Cleary Court there were smiles and the niceties between us. Maisie flung her arms around me and Edward Gowrie was interested to hear about Norway. Mrs G was relieved to see me back to take over the work.

But nothing would sway me now. I put the report in my top drawer. I'd post it the following day. It lay on Mother's silk scarves, like a Judas kiss waiting to be planted on a birth-mother's lips.

⋆　⋆　⋆

FLORA

Owen isn't sitting up beside me drinking the free wine and watching the movie (the first real one I've seen in months). He's hunched up still wearing the TTG tunic with a hideous black coat of Mr Warren-Barnes's over the top and someone's lace-up shoes on his bare feet. Now he's leaning against the window with his lips moving; anyone can see he's praying.

Alan wanted Owen and me out of the country, like immediately! He couldn't come with us because Cristina W-B had been located at last and had refused point-blank to leave. Early the next day we were rushed from the motel to the airport.

Owen had to be wheeled onto the plane. I began to worry about what would happen if he couldn't walk when we got there? And getting him home? If I managed to, it would be like a retriever dropping a half-dead rabbit at its master's feet.

He talked to me a little last night. He feels he's been betrayed by TTG – yet he thinks *he's* betrayed the kids there and Cristina by leaving. He might as well have been in a Russian gulag for all the torture he's going through. When I asked him what it was freaked him at TTG he said: 'You wouldn't understand, Floss.' When I went on about it, he whispered the word *abuse*. Well, funnily enough, I just might understand. I'm pretty hot stuff on abuse by now. Alcohol abuse, domestic abuse and brain-washing abuse, to name a few!

Look, it's not going to be the Hollywood homecoming I've imagined, that's for sure: Ma emptying her last wine bottle down the drain as she takes her beloved son in her arms, Dad throwing his papers into the fire and embracing his boy as his face grows visibly younger like a backwards version of *Crimewatch*, Owen swinging Maisie round and round like they do in reunion scenes. All of this to the smell of home-cooked bacon topped with cinnamon, honey and buttered crumbs.

I've so wanted that.

And how sad will it be when no one is there to meet us? The parents know I'm OK, they've had updates all along, but they don't know that I've found Owen and I'm not supposed to tell them yet. Alan gave me money and the address of some colleagues of his who have said they'll look after us. He wants Owen in good shape before we go home. I sent Patrick a text on the new phone saying when we arrive. But it's nearly three months since the picnic. He's probably got a proper girlfriend by now, not an under-age one with a police record.

When they served dinner I got my brother to take a few spoonfuls of vegetables. He opened his mouth like a baby, then slumped back. He looked so sad I let myself love him a little.

"Hey," I whispered. "You're safe now. Hold my hand!" His was hardly a hand, lost and limp in mine.

★　★　★

At Heathrow I was half leading, half dragging him along when a cart picked us up. After I'd got our case things got worse; Owen shuffled his feet and kept dropping behind. When we emerged from the *Nothing to Declare* exit he slowed to a complete stop and refused to go any further. He sat down, still as a stone, right in the middle of crowds of people and luggage trolleys. I tugged at his sleeve and pleaded . . .

"Please, Owen, Get up . . ."

But he wouldn't move. He sat in a yoga position with the black coat slipping off his narrow shoulders. I stood behind him trying to stop people bumping into him, so they bumped into me instead. I grasped him from behind, and tried to haul him to his feet . . .

"GET UP, GET UP!" I cried.

Suddenly a tall figure in an old mac with rained-on hair was beside us. He took in the situation and, without a word, knelt down and picked Owen up bodily. His eyelashes were wet and there was mud on his boots. They are about the same height, but Owen must have weighed a fraction of what Patrick did.

I followed him blindly, as you would follow a fireman out of a burning building. When we got to his car Patrick laid Owen gently in the back and tucked a rug around him. Then he turned to me. He kissed my face, my forehead, my cold cheeks and the tip of my nose. He helped me into the front seat and put my seat belt on.

The sky was filled with low clouds. A blanket of fog slowed down the cars. The buildings were dirty and the windows looked like strips of used Sellotape – yet it all seemed unutterably beautiful to me. Neither of us spoke.

It isn't Patrick's flat. It's his father's. It's completely grown-up, really posh, with proper furniture, real carpets and one big impressionist painting of women drifting around a garden. It was lovely and warm. Patrick poured us some brandy. Owen stared at his glass as if drinking was something he'd forgotten how to do. I drank mine quickly and suddenly burst into tears.

"You did it, Flora!" Patrick said. "I'd begun to give up on you."

I started to tell him everything, but it came out in an undigested rush. I began at the wrong end with Imogene. I told him about the desert then skipped to the name thing, about how Owen had been given another name and I couldn't find him anywhere, just couldn't. After that I think I described the room with the podium and how scared I'd felt practising the rules.

When I got to that part I shut up because Owen was watching me for the first time, frowning, getting the picture at last.

"They might have kept you," he said slowly. "There are some good people, but they would have been overruled. Thank you for coming, Floss, but you shouldn't have, you shouldn't have come."

"Would you like to sleep?" Patrick asked Owen, exchanging his brandy for a mug of cocoa. Owen drank it slowly and let himself be put to bed on the sofa. There was only one other door going off the big room we were in, apart from the bathroom, his bedroom, of course. I couldn't help noticing that. The brandy hit my stomach like a punch with a warm fist.

Patrick started to make us supper. He looked at a chicken breast doubtfully and reached for a cookbook.

"Have you any rosemary?" I asked, "and lemon? Do you have a lemon?"

"I didn't think you'd know how to cook."

"Too young, you mean?" I said.

Watching him watching me, I tried to keep cool. I'd forgotten the rhythm of his voice. His most ordinary words faze me. And I'd forgotten the way his eyes look into mine. It isn't the normal, look up, smile, look down at what you're doing, sort of thing. His eyes rest in mine, as if looking had no rules.

When I told him about Janie Gospel and the money, he laughed.

"You could be a poker player," he said. "I wouldn't want to be up against you at poker."

The cooking and laughing and the close way we sat together at supper made me think he'd lift me up in his arms and take me through the door into the bedroom. But, after supper, he became formal. He indicated I was to have his bed and ran a bath for me. When I came out after my bath, wearing a T-shirt he'd lent me, I saw he'd organized a sleeping bag for himself on a put-up bed in the space by the window.

"Goodnight, Flora!"

"Goodnight."

I lay down on his bed, wide awake. Every bit of me was alive and hot. I took off the T-shirt. There was a throb in my body and an excruciating longing for an answering throb. I heard the light click off next door and a creak of springs as he lay down. Later, much later, I was still wide awake and still hot, as hot as embers that won't die down. Might he be awake too? I imagined waves of want flowing through the wooden door between us.

Ten more minutes passed. I got up in the dark and stood by the door. I pressed myself against it, then slowly, gently, I pushed. By the light of a cloud-cloaked moon I saw him immediately. He was standing close by the door like me, waiting like me, naked like me.

Wow! Did they ever get it wrong at St Ursula's – all those talks about righteousness? It felt so right! I admit I'd wondered how it really worked. I hadn't understood about the fullness inside you and the way you are moving forward all the time, like a galloping, slowing, quickening horse. I didn't know that every beat would be tangled like a rose with the love in your heart. The beats beating together, so you're laughing and crying at the same time – I hadn't known a girl's body could bend upwards like that, wanting to meet the boy, like a reed wanting sun, and there is more, and more to come, shining hotly down on you both.

★　★　★

I didn't wake up quickly, like I usually do. There was water running in my dream and gradually it turned into the sound of bath water. There was humming in my dream which turned into the hum of buses. I was alone in his big bed. I felt terribly shy and then terribly hungry. After a while I did what they do in books and slipped into the bathroom and washed. I put on the clothes Imogene had given me and went into the other room.

Patrick was finishing dressing Owen, kneeling down, putting clean socks on his feet. My brother sat like an unsmiling child, lifting one foot, then the other.

"Hey!"

They both looked up.

"What about breakfast? We thought you'd have it ready by now." Patrick's voice was firm, but his eyes were smiling. "Make something he remembers," he whispered.

"Do you have any eggs, and tomatoes – and cheese?"

"There's a shop on the corner."

I did everything the way Ma does it. Fluffing up the eggs with a pinch of sea salt, pepper and a teaspoon of water. I peeled the tomatoes and took out the seeds and sliced them thinly. Cheese and tomato omelette used to be Owen's favourite thing. The golden semicircles folded over neatly. The smell filled the room, buttery and nostalgic.

We sat down, but Owen wouldn't eat.

"Mmm," Patrick said.

"Try it, Owen! You used to love it," I said.

He was sitting there like a nirvana-seeking Buddhist – and I'd taken such earthly trouble.

"Mmmmm" Patrick repeated, finishing his omelette.

"Taste it!" I demanded.

"I must go back." Owen muttered, pushing his plate away, lifting a traumatized face to us. "Don't you see? I must go back . . ."

We looked at him, appalled.

MAISIE

Owen! Ma went to school with me, right into my classroom like a girl. She was told to. It was part of Mrs Scott's plan to get me talking. But I couldn't have got a word in if I'd wanted to! First she fidgeted and fussed because her knees wouldn't fit under the desk and Elsie's lot started giggling. Next, in Geography, she corrected the teacher and gave her a lecture on the Basques. There were more laughs. In History she caused a disturbance telling Miss Langley she didn't understand what oppression was. By then the kids were laughing so hard that I laughed too, although my face was red and shining with love for Ma. At the end of the lesson she yawned and made up her eyes.

Aren't they the marvellous eyes, Owen? When she's got them done up she's like a lady on the cover of Elle magazine.

During the lunch break Mrs Scott said it wasn't working, so Ma went home. In the afternoon lesson Annie handed me a message.

"Your Ma's a gas!"

"Thanks Annie," I wrote back.

'She's so not boring!"

"She's not."

"She's like a film star!"'

"Yes."

The teacher separated us but soon a crumpled ball fell on my desk.

"Can I come to your house, Maisie?"

I didn't answer, for my heart was beating like a chaffinch's when it's caught in the pantry. I could hardly breathe for wanting Annie to come. But I was thinking that Ma might be crying that day, or on at Dad – or sleeping. If it wasn't one of Miss Blaine's days there'd be no tea on the table.

Then it happened again – another message.

"Can I come to your house, Maisie?"

I folded it up and put it in my bag. I didn't look up, Owen. I didn't look at Annie. It was drawing class so I did one of Jesus in the Garden of Gethsemane when Peter says "How will we know?" I did Peter with a face like me and I drew flowers in the garden, spiky and foreign-looking. The bell rang and I was still at it. After they were all gone, I ran home.

CHAPTER
10

MISS BLANE

I planned to post the report immediately, but as things turned out I didn't because the very next morning there was a *man* in the house. Not Mr Gowrie, of course not, he's away in the middle of the week now. No, it was a younger man talking to Lila Gowrie behind closed doors. I heard his voice soft and insistent, although I couldn't hear what they were saying. She sounded agitated.

I had a good look at him when he left. He was attractive, as men go, hair too long for my taste, but clean-looking. He was well dressed: a navy sweater – old, but definitely cashmere, and wide-wale corduroy trousers. His shoes were too posh for a worker, yet not posh enough for a lawyer and you'd never see an accountant in leather loafers like the ones he was wearing.

"Next Thursday?" the man said over his shoulder, as he left.

"So soon?" she answered, playfully. Well, it *might* have been playful. It *could* have been playful. He stopped, turned, and looked directly at her.

"Yes, Lila! We have to . . ." Her colour was high. She was nervous, or excited? I couldn't tell which.

"Thursday, then." She agreed, unusually meekly, watching him leave, waiting on the top step until he was out of sight.

It was not the sort of thing you could disregard, not if you're involved, that is. This man could be evidence pertaining to my case.

★ ★ ★

Two weeks later it was Thursday again. It is Thursday he comes, although they've switched to the afternoon. When you think about it the afternoon is a more comfortable time for lovers.

I was almost convinced. What else could it be? *The vixen!* I thought, *the yowling cat!* But, to tell the truth, I was pleased as punch. I'm still holding back my report. The envelope is still in the drawer. A man would be a bonus for me. Eileen could add a man in no trouble at all. *A lover would be icing on the cake.*

Yet I have to admit it's not looking quite right. There's no actual evidence. I've been in after them looking for signs. A pair of scrunched up knickers in a waste-paper basket – or worse. I'd recognise signs, you see. You get them on Hustler TV and all over after 11.30 p.m. But so far there's nothing. The cushions are hardly dented and the rugs haven't the crumpled look you'd expect after moments of passion.

It's disappointing! And I have to admit there's a problem with the sounds – they aren't right either. I listen when he's here. At half three I'm having my tea across the hall. I can't help hearing them, can I? But I haven't heard a single rapt sigh, not a one. I've heard her angry, her smart little boots storm up and down, up and down.

And I've heard her weep, after the weeping there's silence. When he talks again his voice is quiet and steady like before. He leaves punctually at four.

This very afternoon, twenty minutes after he'd gone, Lila Gowrie was off in her car to pick up Maisie to take her to tea with her grandmother. I went into the drawing room to have a look round. There was still no evidence of passion, but I noticed a sheaf of printed-out papers I'd never seen before on her desk.

I walked past and gave them a dusting. 'Nb – *copy for Gavin*' was written on the top one. I went by again and riffled through the papers lightly. My own name appeared once or twice, standing out like black grains in a packet of rice. I was putting them back when a page headed DRINKING caught my eye. Her pen lay across it without the top on. The printer light was flickering . . .

Now, I recognize temptation when I see it, the nuns spelled it out for us at school. I'm not the sort to look at a person's private papers, but this was different. You could say it was my rightful duty concerning the safety of a young child – you could put it like that.

I'll have it back, I thought to myself. I'll have the pen just right . . .

★   ★   ★

DRINKING

FRIDAY:

Alright! When I refused to talk about it you said: 'Write about it.' Well, let me tell you, dear sweet Gavin that you're barking up the wrong tree. I'd rather be doing it than writing about it. I'm not trying to stop. I'm not looking for an elderflower circle of fellow drinkers; I don't want a reformed alcoholic called Harold as a telephone buddy. NO! I like drinking. I positively love it at times – so there!

Is this stream of consciousness enough for you, Gavin? I do hope so. Look, there's something else you ought to know, I don't believe in therapy – well, not this kind anyway. I'm doing this because of that dreary family court. You were a condition, one of my conditions for getting Maisie back. I chose you, as opposed to AA. I mean how could I possibly join AA? You have to want to join. It's the last thing I want.

I'm looking at your first question right now – and, yes, I do have a glass in my hand. How else could I try to answer this stupid question? 'Is there any one thing that could make me stop?'

Well, if you must know, there is one little phrase that affects me. It wasn't Flora who said it to me, not directly; it was Miss Bloodsucking Blane – so why should I care? I don't! But the thing is that it was about her, about my Flo. It was something she might or might not have actually said herself, so it stays in my mind. Ruth Blane told me once that my daughter had run away to find Owen because of me – because she wanted things back like they were: a fire in the grate, me cooking her favourite food and, the interfering old thing added, 'an end to the drinking.'

Let's just say she thought that was the reason Flora left. I doubt Flo said these words. You have to realize my daughter is only fifteen.

Did I say fifteen? Well, she was fifteen when she left. The truth is she's sixteen now. I missed her birthday. You don't have to tell me that's relevant, Gavin. I know it's bloody relevant and, yes, it could be partly my fault, her leaving so young, so terribly young ...

MONDAY:

The weekend was hell! It's all your fault. I don't feel well today and there's something you have to understand. It's to do with Flora's age, she's young, you see. She's too young to know how a mother feels. She doesn't know about drought – or thirst. Look, you don't know her! If you did, you'd know she's a sparkling, adventurous girl – brave, miles braver than any of us, but young. And you wouldn't be able to empathize with a mother like me. You see, she's part of me, she's the good and bad of me, she's my passion, my temper ... my song. This house, Gavin, it has pretty well had it without her here. It's darker now, harder to find your way around.

Don't worry about us. When Flora gets back there will be fires in every room and lemon cake and bacon the way she likes it and, have it your own way, I'll listen to what she has to say.

*I'm amazed by your next question! The **Why do I do it?** question. You are supposed to know these things. They must have taught you something in medical school. Honestly! The need to forget; it's been around for ages. The Greeks had a river for it, Lethe – the river of forgetfulness. And Nepenthe ... wasn't that the potion that chased away Helen's sorrow? Oh, what a heavenly thought! And Coleridge, don't tell me you've never read Kublai Khan? He was right into the forgetfulness thing. He was mad about opium. And kids, Gavin, today's children, the ones with something dreadfully sad in their lives, they have different ways of forgetting. Sometimes they stop eating altogether. Sometimes they cut little notches out of their skin.*

Wine works for me, mostly. When I drink the glare of Owen's absence dims.

If the wine is enough, if I get it right, I sleep away one more night without my son.

★   ★   ★

So he's a therapist! Would you believe it? And one *they've* chosen.
Well, you've to take the good with the bad in this life. A man
would have been *perfect* but, luckily, she's a bad enough birth-
mother without one – and her needing therapy . . . well, it's
helpful, it's *almost* as good.

I put the papers and pen back just as I found them. I was
shutting up that evening when I heard a gasping sound in the
library. I looked in. Edward Gowrie was down on his knees in the
midst of a host of papers ruffling and riffling through them. Now
and then he'd seize one, hold it an inch from his eyes, then cast
it aside. His hair stood on end and his face was purple as a plum.
I thought he was after having an attack and rushed to his side.

"I can't find it, Ruth," he said. "I've looked through
everything, all the early ones, all of them. It's not there . . ."

"Won't you tell me what it is your looking for, Mr G? I'll help
you clear this up . . ."

"No!" He was struggling to catch his breath. "NO, please
don't clear up! I've lost the butter-pat email, her favourite . . .
she's been asking for it."

That makes two of them, I thought . . . crazed! I gave him a
hand up. He sank into his chair breathing heavily. After a few
minutes he seemed calmer. He told me how they'd loved getting
the boy's emails when he was first at college, descriptions of his
friends, all that. In one their son described a prank, something to
do with the young men flipping pats of butter from a tight
napkin onto the ceiling to upset their professor. That's privilege
for you, I thought – childish stupidity! But the idea that he
couldn't find that one silly letter had the man almost in tears.

Black coffee, I decided, and went off to make it. By the time
I got back he'd tidied up a bit and was more or less normal. He

looked at me gravely and said:

"You've seen us through a lot, Ruth, and we are grateful. You must excuse my behaviour tonight. Things have changed. We've had a telephone call from Flora – she'll be home for Maisie's birthday."

"Well, that's nice!" I said. "That'll make you and Mrs Gowrie happy."

"Yes, it will be a great joy, but there was an omission. You see, we've been hoping . . . the young man who has been looking after our daughter gave us reason to hope that her recent journey could result in finding our son. But Flora didn't mention her brother when she telephoned, not once. We were both listening. She would have said something . . ."

As he drank his coffee Mr G told me the time had come for them to face the fact that the lad might not return – "Every avenue has been explored," he said, mournfully. "Statistics! Statistics concerning missing people . . . do you realize 4,000 people go missing every year in Ireland alone? Cliffs over two hundred feet high – and guns . . . my boy hated guns," he murmured, half to himself. "But he knew them. They do, you know, you can't avoid it round here – exposure to guns . . ."

He looked up. The blue in his eyes has faded and his face is unravelling like a bit of knitting slipped off the needle. He's given up, I'd say. He's talking sense at last.

"There, there, Mr G." I patted his hand.

"I must explain to my wife that we have to go on with our lives without him, for the girls' sake. But not yet, not quite yet. I must find that email. It's become a goodnight story, you see. 'Read the butter-pat email, Eddie,' she whispers. The words soothe her. As I read I watch her eyelids lower, then I loosen her fingers and take the glass from her hand. If it's one of the nights she lets me stay I climb in my side of the bed. Just being near her is enough, the proximity of her small movements, the smell of her skin."

He needs rescuing too, if ever a man did. My report's gone now – it's off! When I have Maisie with me, when everything's settled, that is. I'll look after him. I'll have him over and set him by the fire with toast and the tayberry jam he loves. He can keep his books in my bungalow. I'll get a nice bookcase, like the ones they have here. He'll feel at home with Maisie and me. He'll be glad of the comfort.

FLORA

The next day, the following evening, I was still stunned; still feeling his kisses darting through me, inside me, setting off little stabs of pleasure. When Owen was settled for the night, Patrick took me aside and said he had to talk to me urgently. He led me up onto the roof of his building in the freezing cold.

I could tell he was in a state. We'd hardly climbed the steps and he was off: 'We can't do it, Flora! We simply can't make love in the flat again.' It was hard to believe I was talking to last's night's man. He went on – and on. 'He knew I'd agree, out of respect for my brother, out of a sense of decency . . . Obviously! obviously I'd be feeling the same.' I was glad of the darkness. We could hardly see each other's faces. 'For the time being,' he said, 'Owen was our work, our reason for being together.' He paused anxiously, reaching for my arms, gripping them, yet holding me away from him, as if I might come too close and coil myself around him. I didn't speak. I couldn't.

It was baffling. It was agonizing not talking about us, about what had happened after all this time. Last night was still roaring through me like the traffic below, every bit of me blinking on and off like a lit-up hoarding. I must have done something terribly wrong.

"Flora! You do understand, don't you?"

"It's because of me, isn't it?" I asked, eventually. "I mean . . . wasn't it . . . wasn't *I* alright?"

He didn't answer at first – then he reached out and touched my cold cheeks and wound his scarf around my neck.

"Of course it's not about you, Flora. You were wonderful. I'd forgotten. You are so . . . it was your first time, wasn't it? I should have taken better care of you. Listen, darling, it was huge, beautiful, but you see I shouldn't have. Giving in at this point, in my own flat, with your brother there? You must know it was wrong!"

He pulled me to him and stroked my hair. He pressed me against his chest.

"Not wrong," he said gently after a bit, "not any more, just wrong with Owen here."

I couldn't argue although, even as he was comforting me, I felt our bodies align, fitting together like a dovetail joint, warm together in the cold night air. He must have felt it too, for he broke away abruptly and we climbed back down to the flat.

★　★　★

With Owen there all the time a no-touching, no-close-talking wall grew up between us. Patrick was under a lot of pressure workwise, studying for a PhD to please his father. On the days he went to City University I concentrated on trying to make a good dinner. I found one archaic cooking book called: *How to please Master,* but it was all about skinning animals and soaking them in claret – clearly 'Master' didn't eat vegetables and eggs and that's what Owen wanted.

When Patrick got back he included my brother in everything: jokes about my cooking, the news, games . . . We went for walks and tried taking him to a normal Anglican Church, but he walked out in the middle of the service, just walked out and sat on a bench, untouchable, unreachable . . .

Sometimes there was a glimmer of the old Owen, a pencil scribble of his former self, showing interest, smiling at Patrick's stories; but it didn't last. It was as if the sadness was too heavy inside him, thickening around his heart. He used up those days, stole them. I admit I resented it:

"You know you hated TTG, Owen, at least at the end you did. You said so yourself. They weren't what you thought, right? God's supposed to be everywhere, isn't he? And if there is one place he isn't, it's TTG. Do you really think He hangs out in that weird, brain-washing, scary place?

I felt Patrick's hands on my shoulders, holding me back.

"This isn't working Flora!"

"Snap out of it, Owen," I shouted.

"Stop it! Stop shouting! It's no good. We need help."

Patrick grasped me round the waist, pulling me away.

"I can't take him home, like this," I cried.

"I know. I know . . ."

Owen was sitting on the floor, his head sunk on his chest, silently crying. Patrick went over and knelt beside him.

"Don't be afraid," he whispered, rocking him in his arms.

★   ★   ★

We sat in gloomy silence, together and not together. Patrick was reading only the page never turned. I was playing half-hearted patience . . .

"ALAN," he said, suddenly. That's the answer, Flora! We were insane to think we could cope.

"Alan?"

You know, the wonderful chap, your exit man . . .we haven't even been in touch with his colleagues, My God, I've been so irresponsible.

He was right, it made all the sense in the world. It turned out Alan was back from America and vastly relieved to hear from us. He came over the next day and instantly took on board the mess we were in. Owen was visibly calmed by his appearance.

"This happens," Alan explained. "It isn't over yet. It may not be over, for some time."

"But I need to get him home!"

"Look kid," he said to me, hunkering down, balancing on his heels like a dancer, gaunt and intense. "Getting the person out is only part of the deal. Sometimes it works, sometimes it doesn't. Think about it! You have to consider what a person is exiting back into and why he cleared out in the first place."

Patrick asked how long he thought it would take to get Owen well again, but Alan wouldn't commit himself. Patrick then told us that something had come up, and he had to go back to Ireland right away. He said that we could stay on in the flat. I was mystified – and selfish – me alone with Owen?

"It's depressing." I moaned.

"Depressing! You guys don't know the meaning of the word." Alan faced me, exasperated. "Think about it, Owen's not back yet, not in his head. What's happened to my intrepid spy? The great risk-taker? Shape up Flora! Your mission's not over. Have you forgotten why you started all this? Ring your parents. Give them something. Tell them you'll be back for your sister's birthday, whatever. They don't have to know Owen is here yet.

I did what I promised Alan I'd do. I rang Ma and Dad and told them I was safe and said I'd be back for Maisie's birthday. I didn't mention Owen, hearing their voices I was . . . like on the edge of saying 'Help! Come and get us.' I wanted to say, 'I need you. Dad, I give up – I can't cope with my brother any more.' I only just stopped myself in time.

So it turned out that Alan got his way about everything, with one surprising bonus. He was taking Owen to be assessed by a psychiatrist; they wouldn't be back till Monday. Two days, two, before Patrick left. I thought he would be as delighted as I was, but he was looking strange, on edge – unusually spaced out?

★ ★ ★

"Let's run!" he said when they'd gone. "Let's get out of here!" Outside it was late afternoon, the wind chasing a cluster of dark clouds, a pink, watery sun holding on, then petering out, returning in a last wash of fainter colour. We cut down to the river, crossed one of the bridges, and kept going south. By the time we found a place for tea it was dark. I've always loved that, coming out of darkness into light, the clatter that comes with tea, the steamy smell of it, and waiting scones and jam, particularly raspberry jam. Your cheeks unfreeze as you take off your jacket; you are tremendously hungry – but, looking across at Patrick, I saw he hadn't even taken off his coat. He was drumming his fingers anxiously, waiting for me to sit down.

"She's dead," he said, the minute I did.

"What? Who is dead?"

"My mother, Flora. I've known since yesterday. I couldn't tell you with things so bad."

"Oh, no!"

"Yes," He stared at me, as if I could help. He looked bewildered, more than anything else – shocked. "I thought I'd have another chance, you see. I thought there would be a time . . . I was furious when I met her. I didn't have the faintest idea about mental illness then, didn't know it existed . . ."

"That's normal, Patrick."

"Apparently, you can't love people if you haven't been loved yourself. She was a schizophrenic. My father, he sounds devastated – he feels guilty in some way."

"I'm so sorry," I said helplessly.

"She left me something, Flora; a bronze head – my head, and a letter. That's why her friends got in touch. It's how we found out."

We sat in silence, letting o tea get cold. I didn't ask about the letter, obviously. But, after a while, he reached into his pocket and handed it to me without a word.

Dear Patrick,

At least I did one thing that will last. At least I made you. When you burst into my studio like a young lion, full of fury, looking for a mother who wasn't there, I didn't know how to open my arms. I couldn't say the word SON. I wasn't able. After you left I was filled with despair. I sculpted your 'head'. I did it many, many times, Patrick. This is the truest one. I kept it for you.

Now that I'm dying I can say the word at last. In my mind Son becomes Sun. Sunlight streams into my heart. Don't be sad for me. I am not frightened any more.

Forgive me, if you can, dearest boy. I wish I had known what to do. I wish I had stayed.

Your mother, Rose

"It's beautiful," I said. "It shows she wanted to love you desperately, only couldn't. It's about . . ."

"Not sure I can, though."

"Can, what?"

"Forgive her."

"But the letter . . ."

"I know I should, I know she was mad – but she wasn't there, was she?"

"Not there, no." It made me think of Owen. I guessed Patrick was thinking of him, too. Neither of them there – or here.

Patrick looked like he must have at 16, puzzled and hurting, stretching his neck the way young boys do, looking round the room, anywhere but at me.

We walked slowly back in the dark. He let me hold his hand. I felt his sorrow seep into the air around us, like the strains of Mahler's second symphony when it is the sad part and the ache goes right through you.

★　★　★

The following night we got drunk. We'd been close all day, sort of shy together, peaceful and quiet, just hanging out. That evening Patrick was looking in the freezer for ice-cream when he found a big, frosty bottle of Russian vodka, coated with bluish ice. He poured us each a little glass. I tried it, it felt good. The liquid was thick and soothing, it rolled about in my throat. We had a second glass. Patrick seemed freer than he had for ages. And my Owen worries began to slip off by themselves, easy as flip-flops, easy as the top of a bathing suit.

We sat on Patrick's bed, without the glasses, drinking right out of the frozen bottle. Patrick screwed up his eyes and pointed at the level. The level wavered – almost a quarter was gone. "I think, I think he said seriously, they are **here** after all – was **here**, in my mother's case – all the time, just one step away . . ."

The bottle reminded me of the sea, it was as blue and as white as waves.

"You are right" I said, profoundly, sailing on a seamless stream of vodka.

That time was more, even more than before . . . we were sliding up and down an iceberg. I felt the hot of his tongue and the cool of melting snow spilling into us and out of us in one ecstatic flow. We were seals in seal coats, warm together in a vast Arctic Tundra.

"I love you," Patrick said, "and you'll leave . . ."

"I won't, ever."

"There is never an *ever.*"

"I won't go missing from you. Patrick."

"It's alright. This is everything," he said, holding my face, kissing me over and over. "We don't need an ever, just think we have everything now. That's what counts."

★　★　★

So Patrick went back to Dublin and I hung out in the flat getting to know London while Alan worked with Owen. I dyed an elegant stripe in my hair and felt worldly. At first it was grand. One day I got offered ecstasy by a bloke near Ladbroke Road. I didn't have any money so I said no, but it made me feel part of the action. I spent the mornings going to cool shops and trying on designer clothes. It's easy, you dress up and check out the expensive dresses then, when the assistant comes, you say something critical – like you've been looking for that model in a darker shade. Before you know it they are bringing you armfuls of stuff to try. I was only asked to move on once in a bride's shop –

All of that was shortly before I began to feel shallow – really, really, really shallow . . .

By chance I began reading Patrick's father's books. The first was *The Seven Story Mountain* on meditation and attaining inner peace. I tried it, but it didn't work – earthly images wouldn't float past me, they kept catching like a shawl on a ragged nail. Images of the desert, the night the police came to get us with sirens blaring, Imogene's scratched ankles, Owen on the airplane . . . and Patrick, it was impossible to empty my mind of him. I practiced a lot; but only once got the faintest sense of *peace,* a glimpse of what true peace might be like – untrodden land, lit like frost by its own glimmer.

However, that book led to other books. Gradually, I began to realize how useless I was. There were anatomy books too, one marvellous one on the brain. That would be such a fine thing to study, to begin to understand what is happening to Owen, and why; to understand why Rose, Patrick's mother, lost sight of the sun . . .

★   ★   ★

Alan arrived one morning, exhausted.

"What's up?" I asked.

"There's a legal case going on at TTG. They want Owen to be a witness."

"But that's awful. *You* said we could be home for Maisie's birthday. I trusted you!"

"Look, Flora, I'm going to fight it all the way. It won't be easy, but I'll win this one because he's *not* ready."

"You're shite, Alan Corvin." I said in a fury. "I thought you were an exit counsellor and you don't know how to exit anyone from anything. You're giving up!"

"I certainly am not." He was sweating, diving his fingers through his hair. "I'm *not* giving up. I'll never give up on Owen. But now I have to deal with these American fuckers as well. Go home by yourself, if you must."

"I won't!"

"You'd better. You're so young. This whole thing . . ."

"I'm young now, am I? I wasn't young when I was your spy! You're a liar, Alan! You promised, now you're splitting me up from Patrick. Maisie will be counting on us. Ma will drink herself to death before I get there . . ."

"Go," he said. "Bugger off then, if you can't take the heat." We faced each other like boxers, blazing with anger.

MAISIE

Dad and Ma called me into the kitchen. I could tell it was special for they had toasted crumpets and raspberry jam, but before we'd had a bite, Ma said:

"Maisie, dear, come and sit on my knee." I'm big for that – so I didn't. I stood close by.

"Flora's coming back for your birthday, Maisie! Isn't that grand?"

"It is."

Then Dad coughed and looked at Ma and she looked back at him. It was quiet. Ma was squeezing my hand so tight my fingers hurt. Then Dad said:

"Maisie, my little love, you mustn't be disappointed if Owen's not with her. You mustn't count on it."

"Sure and he's coming!" I said, laughing. "Do you not remember the note from Flo when she left? Do you not remember 'Gone to get Owen' on my board?"

But they were off again with warnings and trouble in their faces. After a while I stopped listening and came up here, for they can't help it. They only hear loud noises, not little ones. They don't hear mice in the stubble after the combine's been through or the hush when mist turns to rain. They can't tell if people are close or far.

Owen, I have your bed ready! Miss Blane taught me how to do hospital corners. It's neat as neat. I went to the linen cupboard and found the sheets from great-grandmother Gowrie. They've two O's on them joined like rings for Oriana and Octavius. Just the thing for you. They'll have seen another O coming. You'll be asleep in no time between these sheets. I put your school quilt on top, so you'll be a boy and a brother again.

You'll not know me, Owen. Next week on Thursday I'll be nine!

I'm wearing Flo's old jeans and I have a waist like her ... Miss Blane says it's a figure I'm developing.

Ever since Annie wanted to come to my house she hasn't thrown paper balls or linked arms or shared sweets. But yesterday a ball came fluttering onto my desk. It said:

"D'you fancy Declan, Maisie?"

"Which one is Declan?"

"The one in a rugger shirt."

I didn't know what to say – what with her thinking Ma is like a film star and me not inviting her home. I want her to be my friend.

"I don't fancy yet, Annie." I wrote. I screwed the paper tight and rolled it along the floor.

"Because he fancies you," came back.

You'll tell me how to fancy, won't you Owen? And how to be friends with Annie again?

Ma and Dad haven't put a lock on the door since you left – one push and you're in. You'll be ready for a slice of yellow cake and a long sleep in your bed with the hospital corners after all the travelling.

Dad has the door hinges oiled.

One push is all.

CHAPTER
11

MISS BLANE

I was there when it happened.

"You might as well stay for Maisie's birthday," Lila said to me. "She seems to want you," she added with a half-amused, disparaging shrug.

Couldn't I just claw that woman to death? But I held my peace for little does she know who'll be the favoured one at Maisie's next birthday – and the next. I'd be surprised if *she*'s on my list! I haven't heard from the board yet, but I don't doubt my proposition is under consideration. They'll be going through the legal aspects before they call me in.

The Gowries were expecting Flora back on Maisie's birthday. Flowers! You never saw the like. The whole house was filled with them, great bunches as high as I could reach. And the cooking that went on . . . Mrs G looked the part, alright. She wore a white apron and a chef's cap, a few dark strands of her hair escaped from the cap and clung to her flushed face as she moved between her pots and pans. A bacon joint was roasting in the oven. The smell of foreign spices and some kind of honey billowed outside whenever I was sent to get something from the fridge. She fluffed egg-whites into clouds and tossed tiny dark leaves together with pine nuts and goodness knows what all. Maisie's name was written in stars on a big cake and F L O R A dangled from the ceiling in gingerbread letters. She had Edward, pink in the face, up a ladder looping coloured ribbons through the holes.

Maisie watched the goings on, bewitched.

"We don't know for absolute sure," Edward Gowrie ventured.

"Of course we know! You silly, doubting old . . ."

★ ★ ★

At that moment there was a terrific roaring outside. Cars don't come up to Cleary Court as the drive is overgrown. But there was something coming for sure – crashing through the saplings and nettles, squashing bushes and churning up mud. Edward Gowrie made his way down the shaky ladder stumbling as he landed at the bottom. Lila wiped her hands on her apron, pulled off her chef's cap and stood paralyzed, staring at the door.

Flora came flying into the room. She ran to Maisie first, flinging her arms around her, lifting her up and hugging the life out of her then, reaching for her father, she wrapped the three of them together in another big hug. She's quite the young lady now, her face has fined down. She's slender as a birch sapling, but womanly with it. She's as pretty as one of those celebrities in *HELLO* magazine.

Lila didn't move. I've never seen her that way. The great prima donna with stage fright, at a loss for words for the first time in her life! Flora separated herself from Maisie and looked at her mother.

"Ma! Are you mad at me? Are you?" she asked. "I've missed you so dreadfully."

They stood there, staring at each other. Then the mother reached out and drew her daughter towards her; she moved her hair out of her eyes and smoothed it gently. "*Hija,*" she said. Her hands dropped to Flora's shoulders, she straightened her collar and pulled her closer pressing her cheek against her child's, "*Preciosa*," she whispered.'

"Ma," Flora said, pulling back, "I have a present for you!"

"There's no need for presents, Flo."

"It's not what you're thinking. It's a hurt thing . . ."

"A hurt thing?"

"It will *need* you most of all, Ma. But . . ." and she turned to her sister, her eyes shining, "it's for your birthday, Maisie! And for you Dad – with all my love. And Miss Blane it's just the thing for you, a genuine, knotted-up victim, ready to be unravelled."

"Patrick!" she shouted suddenly – at the top of her voice, "Alan!"

Lila Gowrie stood rooted to the spot – one hand covering her mouth, her eyes fixed on the door. Edward put his arm around her, his face was flushed, his breathing audible. I worried about his heart and wondered where his pills were. Maisie started running, but before she got to the door a creature walked in. I swear to you it was more ghost than man, a veritable skeleton, looking around like a dazed animal, shy of the bright lights.

★ ★ ★

I saw it all. I shouldn't have been there, but I was. I saw the father holding his frail son to his breast and the mother weeping uncontrollably. I saw Flora dabbing her mother's eyes with a dish-towel then leading the boy up to his mother, watching them together, holding her breath. Lila accepted her son, carefully, awkwardly, as if she'd been given something breakable to hold. And he, careful and awkward with her, stood in the circle of her arms like a child wanting to be told what to do next. Neither spoke. Then Maisie was in between them, tugging her brother away, and dancing him round the table. At that moment a buzzer went off and the kitchen was filled with the smell of lemon cake, warm and buttery, sharp and sweet.

"Yellow cake for Owen!" Maisie sang out joyfully. "Time for my Birthday tea . . . "

MAISIE

We were all in!

Flo was sleeping in her room with a grown-up called Patrick. Ma and Dad were sleeping in their room and I was forever checking on Owen. I checked four times. The first time I went in he was on the bed fully dressed, staring at the ceiling.

"Did you not notice the O's, Owen?' I asked him. "It was me that put them there!"

"They're lovely, Maisie! Now go to bed," he said.

I was back in half an hour for I couldn't sleep. My heart was running races and my head was right after it. This time Owen was under the O's, but his eyes were still open.

"Did you hear my voice, Owen? All the time you were gone? Did you?'"

"I knew you were close, Maisie."

"What about Annie, then?"

"Will you tell me about Annie tomorrow?"

"I will."

I was off to bed again, happy. Owen would know what to do. My eyes were half-closing, but the pictures wouldn't stop coming. I went back to his room. His face was calm. His eyes were shut. I stood there.

"Is that you Maisie?"

"It is."

"Well?"

"Will you be out again, Owen? Will you be gone? For we've to clear the garden and I've to show you the new jetty and ..."

"I'm in now, Maisie. I won't leave."

"I saw you sitting on a stone in my dream not knowing which way to go. I think there was an angel there."

"Two, Maisie. Two angels. Flo found me – the other one is called Alan Corvin. He watched over me and brought me home."

"Will you be here in the morning?"

"I will."

"And other mornings? All the others . . . ?"

"I will."

"Goodnight."

"Goodnight."

Late that night I went to his room one more time. The sky was full to bursting with dark, tumbling clouds and the moon was up behind them, pushing them onwards, travelling fast over the wood. I could hear the sea. I knew Owen was hearing it too.

"Hold my hand, Maisie," he whispered.

I took his hand and held it tight till his breathing was even as the tide.

Then I went to bed.

CHAPTER
12

FLORA

Happy Ever After? I don't think so! It was *perfect* at the time, a living dream, a dream we had all dreamt happening in front of our eyes. But it didn't last very long. It seems you bring someone home, have them right there, sitting beside you at breakfast, wanting a five and a half minute egg just like they used to, able to chew and swallow like a human being, but it's all an illusion. He hasn't really landed. Meanwhile we, his cast of characters, are an illusion too, altered, changed in different ways by the waiting, the long, long wait . . . for him.

As for Ma! Oh, it was unbearable at first. She was trying to stop drinking all by herself, sick and sweating, a ghost of the clever, wonderfully funny (with or without wine) person she was. Our poor mother, shy with her own son, aching to please him, while he, the great seeker, the Christian amongst us, the lost and found again Prodigal Son, was no help at all, avoiding talking to her. Off, right after breakfast, to the sea or the monastery or – God knows where he goes – but he's gone all day.

Just looking at them both I hear a splitting sound, like an axe in dry wood. I suspect it's Ma's heart breaking. Without much of a stretch, I'd say Owen's is breaking too . . .

Finally, Ma's therapist organized a drying out place for her, but she couldn't bear to leave. She had to be lifted into an ambulance, hanging on to my neck, dragging me down.

"Keep him here, Flo," she cried out. "Don't let him leave!" As if he were a cat, as if I could put butter on his paws.

★ ★ ★

Now she's back, trying so hard. She's making a huge effort not to drink: cooking for us, trying to squash us back into one family, making plans, like her wedding plan, for instance, her insane idea that we'd all like to go to the Fitz Claybourne's son's wedding. As if! I found her laying out Dad's morning suit. It had the bleached, mothy look of something that's spent years in a box.

"No!" Dad was saying in a tired voice. "I won't wear it, Lila, I won't go."

"But you absolutely must, Edward. It will be fun! Going somewhere again, driving up a drive, drinking champagne, well you can anyway. It will be good for the girls and, well, you never know . . . it could be an inspiration for *him*. I have his good shoes; he'd be alright in a suit . . ."

"No!"

"Eddie, darling, we'll look, like we used to."

"Like we used to?"

"Yes, a SPLASH!"

"A splash?"

"Remember! We used to cause quite a splash."

"I don't splash anymore, Lila.

★ ★ ★

"Flo!" Maisie said to me the other day. "Can you believe it! Owen's a messenger."

"A what?"

"A messenger from God. A sort of soldier angel, I think."

"Yeah? Remind him he's a son too, if you get the chance Maisie."

"I'm not sure they go to weddings."

"Who?"

"Messengers . . ."

"That's nonsense, Maisie! Utter rubbish . . . Owen's still your brother, just a bit madder, not knowing how to fit back, into us, into his family. That's all . . ." I said, weakly, noticing how troubled her eyes were – and the blinking, she never used to blink.

I guess Ma's not the only one who feels she's lost him.

★ ★ ★

The next day I found Ma drifting around the garden. She's always carrying things: trowels, scarves for Dad, seeds, recipes – anything but a glass. I managed to get her to come for a walk with me and started talking about Owen, telling her what Alan had said, about accepting him as he is. She pretended she didn't know what I was talking about. Further on I noticed she was quietly crying.

"What do you mean, Flo? How, how on earth can I? He's far, far away . . . different."

"That's it! You have to get your head round the 'difference,' Ma. You've done so well, giving up booze, all that. You could ask him to help you, perhaps? He loves helping people . . . just don't throw weddings at him – and clothes. He's into the spirit, not shoes."

By this time we were at the bay. Ma gazed at the sea for a long time. She hasn't swum for years. "Let's." she said suddenly. "Come on!" Leaving a little pile of her clothes, far too near the edge, she rushed into the freezing water. I followed and saw her wobble and disappear completely for several minutes, swashed away by the first big wave, only to emerge further out, laughing, her frail arms flailing, ghost legs swept behind her like scarves; "The spirit!," she shouted out as she vanished again under another wave. "Thank you, Flo!"

I wondered how I'd ever get her in . . .

★　★　★

Then there's Patrick, or rather then there *isn't* Patrick. Patrick postponed . . . Patrick over? I can hardly believe it. The extraordinary thing is Owen is the one responsible. It began in London, the day I came back drenched from escaping the man on a barge. Owen didn't advise me, heavens no, I wouldn't have listened if he had. It was more a case of him slowly making me think about 'what's next?' He did it with books really, if putting the right book in front of a very frightened person counts as saving them from themselves?

The day of Maisie's birthday, the day I brought Owen home, well, that was the night things went terribly wrong between us. I'd been longing for Patrick. Imagining him with me, on my bed, close again, but it turns out I made a massive mistake. In fact, we both made massive mistakes. I plunged headlong into telling him how I'd decided to study flat out – to catch up – to *be* someone. I explained I'd never be able to help anyone if I didn't. I even gave him a list of the things I've planned to achieve. I'd thought he'd be rejoicing with me but, when I looked at his face, his was retreating. He looked like someone walking backwards out of the room you are in . . .

"No! Flora, no," he interrupted, "You've got it all wrong. I love you. We can be together now – openly! It's *our* time . . And

198

he began to pour out *his* plans, for *me*. Me following him to Amsterdam where he's starting his first job. Me decorating our first flat. Me cooking and getting to know the rest of his family.

We looked at each other aghast. We were on totally different planes. I didn't want to hurt him like his mother had – and he didn't want to hurt me, so we tried desperately to get it together. . . in the end we made guilty love. That was a fatal mistake. He held me fiercely in a 'you're mine – sign here,' sort of way. I hated it. Even our words came out wrong; they swerved about like bats in the dark.

Patrick left the next morning.

We do love each other, but platonically for now. I don't see why it couldn't work. A noble, poetic love, like the Greeks, had no sex or cooking, no having to be home by six.

MAISIE

I thought I'd ask Dad about my new school and tell him about
Ma not going to the parents' meeting and me needing a house
tie. I was going to tell him about Ma's friends' grand wedding
and how I'd love to go too, except my dress has got so short . . .

But Dad's tired now, and he doesn't sew. He's fine! Of course
he's fine. He loves sitting and looking at us and knowing
everyone is here. And he loves reading his bird books and looking
up things up in his bird dictionary. The trouble is his eyes shut
by themselves, they just do! Then they flip open and he says,
"What was that, darling?" So you have to begin again. His skin
has dried into little crossroads and his neck has loosened. When
he hears my voice he pats the arm of his chair for me to sit on. I
love being with him. I make tea for us both. After a few tries I
decided it was better just being there. I didn't tell him about my
dress.

Next I asked Flo. She was on her computer and said: "Yeah,
yeah, Maisie, I'll take you shopping soon." "When?" I asked. She
told me not to bother her as she was filling out an application
form and, when I asked what that was, she said: "If I don't apply
now I'll be stuck in this Goddam place forever." I was sad,
because Flo's voice was cross. I went up to my room. After a bit
more feeling sad I decided to tell Owen. He wasn't here, but I
told him, anyway.

Owen! Everything's moving so fast, like we are all in a film,
Nobody stops to tell me things, and I can't find anyone to listen.
You see I'm better now, mostly, but for secondary school I'm
going to need different socks and a house tie, and a grey blazer.
There was a meeting when they told parents what we need, but

Ma didn't go. She said she knows a better place, but we haven't been to the better place. You see, Owen, since my brother, I mean you, I mean now that he . . . you . . . came back, and became a messenger from God, Flo says: 'We are in a hell of a muddle.' Ma, wants us all to go to a posh wedding. I *want* to go! I have a beautiful dress, but it needs letting down. And Miss Blane, Owen, the big lady who used *always* to be here, isn't here any more . . . Ma says: "Thank the Lord for small mercies," Flora says: "You don't want to know, Maisie." but no one will tell me where she went. And no one else lets things . . .

"Who are you talking to, Maisie?"

Owen was standing right there, on my carpet, in my room. I felt so silly. My cheeks were blushing red and hot with how silly I felt.

I couldn't speak.

"Was it easier talking to me, Maisie, when I wasn't here?"

I stood still. My voice wouldn't work . . .

"Maisie – I'm so sorry."

"It's because you are a messenger now," I said. "I didn't want to bother you – about my dress being too short, and the house tie and what Flo said about you forgetting to be a son. And about Miss Blane, not knowing where she went. And Owen, and nobody else lets things down or looks over the school list and, poor Ma, she hasn't had time and . . ."

Owen stared at me, then he said: "Let's go for a walk and a talk, Maisie Moo. We'll sit on our bench, shall we? We'll try to unmuddle the muddle. Bring your school list and your dress. I'll bring a needle and thread."

Then we just stood there, quietly. And Owen held out his hand:

"I'm very sorry, little M."

FLORA

I'm off in 8 days, accepted, at last, by a brilliant tutorial place in Edinburgh!

And, dare I say it? Things are better. The swimming must have brought Ma's courage back, because yesterday she *tackled* Owen. She literally blocked his way out of the kitchen in the narrow passage that leads to the garden. She did it like a rugby player, standing right in his way!

He moved to one side. She moved to block him. He stood in the middle. She stretched out her arms, touching both sides of the wall. He made a pass to the left. She was there before him. I could just see the back of my brother's long hair and Ma's dark eyes fixed intensely on him. When I peeked again Owen was laughing, walking straight into her open arms. For the rest of the day they were together, sitting on the grass, walking, laughing and crying. I think there was a bit of that too.

Maisie seems to have stopped idolizing Owen and is back to dragging him around. She's pretty normal now – teenage normal, listening to music, wearing my clothes, covering her diary in a sort of body hug if someone comes into the room.

No, the hardest one to leave is Dad. I wouldn't say he is unhappy, just closing down. I suppose it's alright to only remember the good things in life? But it's as if Owen never left and I never found him. The other day I mentioned Arizona and he said: "How lovely, did you go there for a holiday?" He doesn't want to talk about America, or his terrible journeys looking for Owen or Ma's drinking or Maisie being put in care . . . if you try to talk seriously his eyes close. You can tell he'd rather not talk about any of it. He doesn't go to the marsh any more to watch sea bird and waders, he's content to look them up in his book. When he's asleep, the heavy book slips to the floor and one of us picks it up. Later when he finds the right page and finds the birds he is delighted all over again.

It's alright, of course. I love him being happy. But sometimes I feel jealous, like the Prodigal Son's brother who was tilling the fields when he was away. So far as Dad goes, Owen never left – and I never tilled . . .

RUTH BLANE
A year later

It wasn't long after the boy came home that I got an answer to my letter at last, from the head office of Social Care Services. I walked to the centre, with all the hope in the world. It seemed to me that the timing was just right, Now that her precious boy was back Lila wouldn't have time for Maisie anyway.

But, the minute I saw my four inquisitors lined up, and the empty chair waiting for me in front of them I realized they were out to get me. On their desks were copies of my reports, and copies of the copy I had made of Maisie's passport and copies of my letter to them. *The letter,* the most important in my life, putting myself forward as Maisie's foster mother was there too; covered with angry black markings.

Their accusations went on and on: reports inconsistent with the truth, the slanderous way I talked about my employers, outright blame for the time Maisie was left alone. Words like unstable, unsuitable, and untruthful were bandied about and, after describing me as a dangerous woman who'd slipped through the net, Mrs Scott dared to suggest that my feelings for Maisie were inappropriate.

I knew I'd had it. My career, my successes, my dreams for a life with Maisie were all over. And, most terrible of all, I wasn't be allowed to see her – there was to be a barring order out on me. I couldn't go to her school, couldn't go to the house or the vicinity. 'Did I understand the word *vicinity*?' Oh, Mary mother of God, yes I did: the bay, the ice-cream shop, our secret wood, the paddling river . . . But, by then, I'd stopped listening. All I could see was Maisie's trusting face. All I could feel was her little hand in mine.

How did it end? I don't remember an ending. I was back in the flat, feverish, sick and out of my mind for weeks on end . . . and *she* was back too. . . I couldn't sleep for the whine of her chair and the screech of brakes as she stopped it outside my room.

'Braat? I know you're in there. Bra aat.'

I learned later if it hadn't been for Edward Gowrie I'd have gone to prison. His intervention was included in my dismissal papers. He was quoted as saying: '*I refuse to be a witness. Ruth Blane's maternal affection for my daughter was understandable in the circumstances.*' It was him, too, sent Dr Jane Stephens all the way from Cork to get me well again. I told her about the flat being haunted and, next thing I knew, they were painting the whole flat and Mother's dummy with her cloth smirk and sawdust breasts was out on her neck at last. He must have paid for that.

Eighteen Months Later

'I was near spending the money I got from Aunt Minna, the money saved for the day Maisie comes looking for me. I'd never touch that so what could I do but start working again. I had Mother's machine, after all, and a new modern dummy, pleasant and plastic without a face. It wasn't hard to get going. I sent a letter out to Mother's old clients and got their favoured Earl Grey tea in . . .

There were enough of them – customers – chatting and changing their minds, wanting a tightening here and more bosom there. I wasn't interested in their goings on. I didn't listen.

Until one day I was fitting a lady for an evening skirt. She was talking ononon to her friend about a concert they'd been to. I was down on my knees concentrating on the measurements, when I couldn't help hearing the words:

"Wasn't that Edward and Lila Gowrie's youngest daughter?"

"I believe it was," my client answered, "A voice like an angel! I'm not surprised they chose her for the solo."

"I thought my niece, Helen, would get it, but they wanted the Gowrie girl." The friend said in a sulky voice.

I stood up slowly. My knees were shaking, my mouth was dry, yet I'd a yearning to say her name out loud, I wanted them to know . . .

"Would it be Maisie Gowrie you're talking about?" I asked.

"Do you know her?" my client asked.

"Indeed I do! I'm her . . . I took care of her, you see – I'm her . . . guardian."

"But, wasn't she the child with a disability?" The annoying one persisted.

"Oh no! that was a childhood thing . . . she was helped, you see, professionally."

"Well, she's certainly made up for it now!" my client said. The child has a lovely voice, hasn't she?"

Humiliation reddened my neck and rose to my cheeks. A lovely voice? I had not known. I, Ruth Blane, had not even known. I felt proud – and possessive.

"Maisie was always a great one for a song," I answered a little too loudly," starting to clear away, putting the pins hurriedly back in the box.

Finally, I got them to leave with another lie that dropped out of my mouth at the last minute, a painful, wistful, dishonest lie which came out in an unnaturally high voice. "Time's up, I'm afraid," I said. "I have her tea to make, you see. She usually drops in on her on her way back from school."

★ ★ ★

I put the chain on the door, switched off the lamp and sat down. Slowly, the flat filled up with music, the sound of Maisie singing, a sound that never once I heard in all those years. Maisie! Out there in front of an audience, the governors and the whole school. My Maisie, with that woman and her kind in the crowd.

How could it be?

The room grew dark and the hour grew late. I was still sitting there at midnight, wondering what it was changed us all, when of a sudden, the answer came to me, clean and clear at last.

It's only now I see that the boy was never gone. He was there in every glass of liquor that Lila Gowrie drank and there, too, in the silence Edward Gowrie kept. He was the burned-down fire and the grown-over garden and it was because of him the cupboards were empty and no tea on the table when the girls got back. He was the sweet ache in their music and the howl of pain in their fights. It was for the boy's sake the front door swung open at night and the wind and the rain let in. Owen Gowrie was the fire in young Flora's head that drove the child to leave her family to hunt her brother down. And Maisie, little Maisie Gowrie – for sure it was his absence stole her voice away, and his coming home set it free again.